ENLIGHTENMENT

David Berardelli

ENLIGHTENMENT

GRAVESTONE PRESS

Gravestone Press
is an imprint of
Fiction4All
www.fiction4all.com

This Edition
Published 2022

Cover Art: Linda York

PART 1

Chapter 1

Her hands feverishly gripping the wheel of her Honda Accord, Lynn Monroe reached downtown Wheeling shortly after seven that evening.

She was surprised she'd made it without killing herself or someone else. Eastbound traffic on I-70 proved as horrendous as usual, the rush hour bursting with excitement and continuous close calls. In this case, it was Friday—which made things even more chaotic. The highway remained frantic with not only evening rush, but also party-goers anxious to begin their long-awaited Friday night celebrating.

But she'd made it, and even though she had to pry her frozen fingers loose from the wheel after parking the Honda, she reminded herself that she'd managed to cover the last fifteen miles in less than fifteen minutes. And without killing herself or adding to the pandemonium.

Nevertheless, the evening had been traumatic. Just thirty minutes earlier, she'd closed up her poster shop in downtown St. Clairsville, driven the three short blocks to Frank's townhouse and walked in unannounced.

And witnessed the unspeakable horror that had just taken place with her boyfriend and her younger sister Ariana.

She cursed herself once again for coming all this way in the first place. And cursed Frank. And

5

Ariana. And life and its inconvenient grab-bag of unpleasant surprises.

Her plan had been to leave The Poster Shoppe a few minutes early. Since Jodi, her assistant manager, also had weekend plans, she'd agreed wholeheartedly with Lynn's strategy. It was a no-brainer for either of them to close up shop for the day and transfer the money from the cash register to their small office safe. Lynn had originally wanted to head on over to her apartment, change into something sexy, then drive over to Frank's for a little fun and frolic before they went out for their usual Friday night candlelight dinner at one of the better steakhouses in Wheeling.

She had no idea that her big plan would hit a major snag when she decided to drive straight to his townhouse instead. Frank had said something recently about her not being spontaneous, that she always planned everything in advance. She needed to be more impulsive. More carefree.

So, after some serious thought, she'd decided to challenge him and prove him wrong.

She didn't expect to see Ariana with Frank in his townhouse. And she certainly didn't expect to see them both scrambling for their clothes once she'd let herself in, walked down the carpeted hall and opened his bedroom door.

Her hands were still numb from clenching the wheel as she sat in her car next to the curb a few spots down from a well-lit hardware store. It took considerable effort to let go of the wheel and a few painful minutes to restore circulation in her damp

6

fists so she could switch off the ignition and the lights.

Afterward, she sat back for a few minutes to get her breath. Her heart still raced—an extremely unpleasant combination of anger, humiliation and shock. Her thoughts scurried by at an alarming rate, but she soon found that if she focused on the present, she would eventually be able to think clearly. And as she sat in her dark cocoon of misery, staring numbly at the hordes of people rushing by, she struggled to keep from thinking about what she had to do.

Her struggle was very brief. In spite of focusing on the here and now, she just couldn't switch off the dark images racing past.

The relationship was over; that much was painfully clear. She couldn't possibly stay with Frank Alden after what he'd just done with her sister. The images of them scrambling to cover themselves would never leave her, and she was certain that these awful pictures would most likely stay with her for the rest of her life.

But as angry as she was with her sister, she realized she couldn't put all the blame on her. Ariana was slender and beautiful, and, at twenty-three, just as silly as she'd been in high school. She also possessed an air of naivete that had never failed to stop a man—any man—dead in his tracks. And her large emerald green eyes had always been her most devastating weapon in her impressive arsenal.

However, she could easily blame Frank. The man was thirty-eight and as savvy as they came.

7

Managed a Hedge Fund. Drove a shiny black BMW. Owned a townhouse worth half a million, easy. His fifty-thousand-dollar wardrobe, along with his sophistication and charm, had always been his pride and joy. He was divorced, but that had been years ago. And as he'd stated so many times to so many people, he'd learned many things about females ever since.

In other words, Frank knew better. At least, he *said* he did.

However, he certainly didn't demonstrate his philosophy very well.

Suddenly exhausted, Lynn leaned back against the padded headrest. A wave of sadness washed over her, and she began to sob quietly.

***

Once the storm raging through her had subsided, Lynn opened her handbag and pulled out a Kleenex to wipe away her tears and begin the arduous chore of repairing her face.

Even in the best of conditions, such a task quickly became frustrating and seemingly impossible. Never having been considered ravishing, she'd always been regarded as pretty-- even pleasantly attractive—once she'd gotten her color tones just right and applied the correct touch to her cheekbones. But no matter how terrific her makeup and hair ended up, she knew she'd never reach the level of "striking" or even "mildly stunning" that most of the women she'd known in school and in college took for granted.

Even so, she'd managed to turn a few male heads since graduating from high school nearly fourteen years ago. And although she wasn't what most men could call a genuine "babe," she knew she had much to offer in a relationship. She was intelligent, honest and faithful, and had never been one to listen to idle gossip or base her personal evaluation on someone else's opinion. She'd always been slender, looked pretty good in her tee shirts and jeans, and had been told many times that her light-green eyes actually sparkled when she smiled.

I might not smile for quite a while... She frowned at her blotched reflection in the small round mirror she'd removed from her makeup case and found herself growing angry again. She applied a light coat of lipstick and blotted her cheeks with the makeup brush to hide the anger and the hurt, hoping to create at least an illusion of happy.

The very thought of such nonsense gave her the impulse to laugh. Right now, happy would be a serious stretch. In fact, something even as mild as a pleasant smile would now be just as unattainable as anything she'd ever lusted after. Thanks to Frank and his uncontrollable hormones, she doubted that she'd be happy—or even slightly content—for many years to come.

In her view, it was frightfully obvious that Frank Alden didn't care what made her happy. In fact, it was painfully apparent that the man was concerned only about things directly related to him and his immediate needs.

But at least I care about me...

She shuddered as a fresh onslaught of heated anger sliced through her. *I care about my face. And about myself. And I really should, because I'm me. And like everyone else, I'm unique. There is no one like me anywhere in the universe. But it's now painfully obvious that no one cares about me as much as I do.*

Why change anything about you? some strange inner voice asked as she slipped the makeup brush back into its case. *Frank isn't here. Why reward him for what he's done? Why reward him at all for anything?*

That made perfect sense. Her present state of misery was, in actuality, a crude way of rewarding him for his indiscretions. Putting him in charge again. Making his actions feed her destruction.

She needed to have fun. To be in charge of her own life. Like Frank—and, obviously, Ariana—she had to be a little indiscreet herself. And she intended to do just that.

Now was the perfect time, while she was in the mood.

Once she'd finished with her face and hair, she decided to head down the street, where the big white sign, PECO'S, flashed brightly above the bar entrance.

Chapter 2

At 7:30, the place wasn't quite packed.

Several small groups of giddy folks followed Lynn inside. All but four tables and two or three barstools in the large smoke-filled room were filled. Half a dozen couples moved awkwardly on the dance floor on the opposite end of the room, groping one another. A heavy pulsating number grumbled angrily from the juke, barely audible above the clinking of glasses intermixed with drunken laughter, catcalls, and hysterical shouting.

Lynn chose a vacant stool near the end of the bar, about ten feet from the door. Assessing the crowd, she quickly saw that there wasn't anyone she wanted to connect with. Everyone was either already half-drunk or staggering, and the few men she saw acting reasonably sober were chatting with their dates.

She decided to stay close to the door just in case immediate escape became necessary. She wanted to appear as invisible as possible. This wasn't her type of place, but she didn't want to spend the rest of the evening wandering the streets, looking for a more appropriate place. The few really great bars she knew of operated from the best restaurants, but she wasn't appropriately dressed—or hungry—for fine dining.

So, for the next few minutes, she ignored the glossy smiles of the half-drunk men sitting on stools next to her and waited for the redheaded bargirl to come over.

A few minutes later, Lynn ordered a vodka tonic. While waiting for her drink, she subtly scanned the crowd in the reflection of the large bar mirror on the other side of the counter.

The room consisted mostly of males in their thirties and forties. Blue-collared men obviously here to spend their paychecks for fun and as much drunken mindlessness as they could manage. In their outlandish colors and tight, revealing clothing, the women hanging around the men were probably hookers. Lynn counted eight of them. Four girls sat at the bar, sandwiched between the men and joining in with their drunken chatter. The others occupied tables and flirted with future prospects.

Lynn's drink came. She dropped a five on the counter. The redhead scooped it up and went back to the register to ring it up.

The drink was strong. She had a small sip and promised herself she wouldn't have another. One more of these would make it impossible for her to drive back to St. Clairsville without killing herself or someone else along the way. She'd never been a heavy drinker and preferred a glass of white wine with her meals. She just didn't want to draw attention to herself by ordering anything someone would consider bizarre, coaxing them over for silly conversation and drunken flirting.

But after thinking about it for a few moments, she wondered if she should have ordered the wine anyway. This was, after all, a special occasion.

Well, wasn't it?

She almost smiled at the phrase. That certainly was a weird term for whatever this situation was. Special occasion. Sounded almost proper, if you didn't have any idea what was actually going on.

In reality, this was nothing more than denial on her part. Turning her back on what she'd seen in St. Clairsville. Leaving the scene of a despicable act. Shutting down and turning away from the one thing she never ever wanted to see. Closing her mind on the image of her boyfriend having sex with her kid sister.

I'm an idiot. The very thought of it made her want to scream. *I should have killed both of them while I had the chance.*

Her hand shaking, she raised the glass to her lips. Yes. Idiot was an appropriate term. She'd observed the awkward scene in excruciating silence, but instead of confronting them, or roaring like a wounded lioness, or grabbing the nearest butcher knife and slitting their throats, she'd turned right around and ran out of the room.

Had she really done such a silly, cowardly thing? Or had she blurted out something right then that clearly reflected her outrage?

She couldn't remember. Thinking about it now, she realized that she might have indeed said something. She might have gasped. Or brought her hand up to her mouth. Or muttered something like, "Seriously?" Or, "My God!" Or even, "I can't believe *any* of this!"

13

But all she could remember was the shock of watching them scrambling for their clothes.

Then, after the horror of the event had ultimately worn off, reality returned, telling her that she really shouldn't be standing there, watching them. It was no place for her to be. And nothing good would result from her spending one more second in that townhouse.

She'd immediately turned around and rushed outside, jumped into the Honda, got onto I-70, and drove away.

She'd escaped. Vanished. Turned her back on both Frank and her sister. Turned away so she wouldn't let the cursed image develop more vividly in her head. And, possibly, to give them time to consider what they'd done. And the impact it had made on her. And how much they'd truly hurt her.

But as she thought about it now, she could only wonder if she'd done the right thing.

But what *was* the right thing?

Should she have gone ballistic? Scratched Frank's eyes out? Kicked him in the balls? Strangled Ariana until her eyes popped out of her skull? Pummeled her to the ground? Rushed outside and yelled bloody murder?

Lynn had never been the violent type. For her, denial had always been preferable to acting out her frustrations. Turning away worked wonders. Or closing her eyes. Or taking a breath and walking away. This had been her code of conduct ever since she could remember. Even in the worst-case scenario, she'd always been able to visualize the results of whatever dilemma she'd faced. To imagine what could happen if things escalated.

What would have happened if she'd gone primeval and resorted to the attack mode? Would someone have died? Frank or Ariana would have certainly been gravely injured, the paramedics most assuredly called in.

Then what? A charge of aggravated assault? A prison sentence? A permanent scar on her spotless record? A future filled with people staring at her as she walked down the street? Endless whisperings? Fear? Contempt? Anger? Suspicion? The media parked outside her condo? Reporters flocking her each time she showed her face? Small crowds gathering outside the store? Customers afraid to come in for fear of being interviewed?

As she thought more about this, she realized that in spite of her initial reaction, she'd actually done the right thing. Instead of making things worse for herself, she'd simply turned away from Frank and walked right out of his life.

Ariana was a different story entirely. Ariana was her kid sister and, as everyone knew, sisters stayed close to each other forever. It had been an unspoken bond for centuries. A natural element everyone actually believed. And only something as powerful as death could sever this bond.

But what happened to the bond when one sister betrayed the other by venturing into forbidden territory?

Ariana had always been the princess in the family. The prettier of the two. The daughter everyone noticed, envied, doted over. The girl everyone in town always thought would become a model, or movie star. Or wife of a doctor. Or rock star.

Lynn, as most everyone knew, was smarter, more sensible, and infinitely more mature than her younger, prettier sibling. Lynn was the daughter any parent would be proud of. A girl who would carve a career for herself through hard work and perseverance. Solid. Steady. Always staring straight ahead, without a sideways glance to take her eyes off her goal.

A man would come into her life one day. But until that day arrived, she would be immersed in her career and would not even consider such a distraction. And if—or when—such an event took place, she would instinctively know how to prioritize it.

Suddenly disgusted with herself, she had another tiny sip of her drink. Then, knowing she was wasting her time in this loud, foul-smelling place, she slipped down from her stool and left the bar.

As she went back out into the cool night, she knew she had to resolve this dilemma somehow. She had to approach both of them. Confront them. Tell them how much they'd hurt her. How they'd messed everything up. They no doubt knew that already but had to actually hear it coming from her to fully realize the consequences of their actions.

You've yanked out my heart and stomped on it. She knew she needed to tell them those very words.

16

You've destroyed my love for both of you, and you've taken my trust and tossed it where I'll never be able to find it again.

They had to know this. And they had to hear it from her the moment she drove back to St. Clairsville.

But just as she approached the curb to cross the street, heavy footsteps came up quickly behind her.

***

"Wanna party, baby?"

Feeling as if her body had just been doused in ice, Lynn spun around. Two large, sloppy-dressed men in their mid-thirties stood unpleasantly close, grinning stupidly at her. The heavy stench emanating from them smothered her and she had to force herself not to gag. The man on her right was the one who'd just spoken. He was more than half a head taller than her, making him around six-two. He had piercing dark eyes, dark features, and a scraggly black beard. Dressed in a leather jacket, jeans and biker boots, he wore no shirt, exposing an extremely hairy chest. Lynn could tell instantly that he hadn't been near a shower stall in days.

"Time to party," said the other one with a smirk. He was just an inch or so shorter than his friend, but just as wasted, and emitting his own equally strong cocktail of B.O., whiskey, and foul breath. His features were not nearly as dark as his friend's, and his beard looked more like uneven stubble than anything else. He wore a light-gray sleeveless sweatshirt, jeans, and cowboy boots. A do-rag covered his head. Long, scraggly blondish

17

hair emerged from the bottom of the rag, settling in matted clumps over his shoulders.

Lynn strongly feared that she was in serious trouble. But she knew that the worst thing she could do was panic.

"Listen, guys," she said, surprised that her voice was working, "I appreciate the offer, but—"

Both men chuckled.

"Offer?" The second one winked at his buddy. "Hear that, Smoke? We found ourselves a classy one tonight!"

"We'll see how classy she be," Smoke said. "Once we take her to the Holler, git her nice'n wasted, she'll loosen up!"

Her pulse thumping wildly, Lynn glanced to her right. Heavy traffic continued in a steady stream. On her left, a mailbox sat next to a parked SUV. Her only escape route rested between the two men. But since they were standing just two feet apart, she realized she couldn't possibly slip through them without them grabbing her.

Dammit, Frank Alden, she thought angrily, *if I manage to get out of this alive...*

The two of them simultaneously reached out and grabbed her arms. She tried pulling away, but they were strong and held her easily. Panic set in. She realized she was completely helpless. Then, just as her mind went blank, they turned and half-dragged, half-carried her down the block leading to the dark, foul-smelling side street separating Peco's from another building.

18

She was too weak with fear to resist or even work up an impressive scream. Her inner sense told her that a scream would infuriate them. They were obviously very drunk, and she knew from personal experience what could happen when two big, rough men faced frustration during a drunken binge.

Her heart fluttering, she held her breath and wished herself in a different place. She knew that was impossible, even silly, but her thoughts had slammed into overload and she could hardly control them. As they hauled her forcibly down the street, she hoped and prayed that she could survive this night. She also hoped she could live long enough to see her sister and Frank once again. It was now more important than ever that they fully realized how much they'd hurt her and that they'd literally forced her into a horrible nightmare. They hadn't *caused* this, but if it hadn't been for what she'd caught them doing, she wouldn't be here in the first place.

Just as she began thinking of a feasible escape plan, they'd reached an old Chevy pickup parked in an isolated spot at the end of the alley, near a dumpster overflowing with trash and rotting food. Without a word, they yanked open the passenger door and forced her into the front seat. The one in the leather jacket called Smoke got behind the wheel. His buddy squeezed in next to her and pulled the passenger door shut. Then, while settling into the seat, he chuckled and draped his left arm around her shoulders. She found herself enveloped in a horrendous cloud of nauseating B.O.

Lynn lowered her head and breathed in through her mouth. Her pulse hammered loudly as Smoke gunned the truck and slammed it into reverse. A moment later, they'd backed out into the street and crept up to the intersection. Ignoring passing traffic, they pulled right out.

For the next half-dozen lights, Smoke snaked the pickup in and out of the heavy Friday night traffic. Judging by their direction, Lynn could tell they were heading toward Bridgeport.

"Got us a live one, Shine." Smoke rubbed her thigh as he manned the wheel with his free hand.

"She may not be smokin' hot," Shine said, grinning and looking her over, "but she sure as hell's got the right stuff."

"They all do." Smoke pulled between another pickup and a dark sedan. He lit a cigarette from the crumpled pack he'd snatched from his inner pocket.

"Mebbe." Using his free arm, Shine bent forward to search for something underneath the seat. He raised his arm and the stench grew even worse. He was holding up a large bottle of whiskey. "But this one's got what we want most."

"Whazzat?"

Shine shrugged. "She's right here!"

They both howled laughter.

Lynn shivered and forced herself to stay focused. And kept breathing through her mouth.

She prayed that she'd somehow survive this night.

20

Chapter 3

Ten minutes later, they reached downtown Bridgeport.

Shivering with fear, Lynn strongly suspected that these two were going to rape her. She also realized that if this were true, she'd have to make a very important decision very soon. However, whatever decision she made would not necessarily be a good one. Or even a safe one.

But even so, she had to do *some*thing. Whatever it was, it had to be done while she was still able to function. If they knocked her out or tied her up, she'd be totally at their mercy. Then she'd be forced to face the terrifying fact that she might not come out of this alive.

The two men remained silent as Smoke made a right onto another harshly-lit street. Shine sipped the whiskey from the bottle as they eased down the block in the heavy traffic. He handed the bottle to Smoke, who sucked down a quick gulp. After a loud belch, Smoke offered the bottle to Lynn, who shook her head. "Ya sure, baby? Damn good hooch. It'll make ya hot and wild inside."

"Wild's fine, eh, baby?" Shine winked at her and grinned stupidly.

"Yup." Smoke smacked his lips and fired up another cigarette. "Wild's just fine and dandy. I like wild. Turns Junior on like nothin' else."

"Hot, too," Shine added. "Don't forget hot, Smoke."

21

"Ya got *that* right..."

They both laughed and swatted her on the thighs.

Lynn winced at the stinging pain and nervously watched the busy street. With both windows down, she should be able to belt out a good scream to let someone know she was in serious trouble. Maybe someone would even grab their cell and call 911. Anything would be better than sitting here wedged between these two in this filthy seat, waiting for the inevitable.

However, the figures she saw wandering down the street didn't even turn in her direction.

She had to face the frightening conclusion that anonymity might actually be a better choice. The heavy, sour-smelling arm draped across her shoulders nauseated and intimidated her, strongly suggesting that any effort to bring attention to them would result in excruciating pain.

Shine gulped down more whiskey from the bottle. He shoved his bulky frame closer and let his forearm cover her left shoulder and upper arm. His large hand slid down her front, stopping just above her left breast. Sensing disaster, Lynn forced herself not to throw up. She shrugged in an effort to persuade him to move his hand. It remained where it was. Taking a slow, deep breath, she tried again. His hand moved closer, until the palm covered her breast. Her heart pounded. She squirmed and tried raising her arm. Chuckling, he moved his face closer. "Like that, baby?"

She struggled to ignore his putrid breath singeing her cheeks. "Not now. Not...here." Hopefully, he'd take that as something to look forward to and not cold rejection.

"Plenty a time for that later on," Smoke said, snickering. "Ya git 'er all worked up and squirmin' around, I won't be able to concentrate on my drivin'..."

Shine pulled his hand away and focused once again on the whiskey.

Lynn sighed in relief and waited for her heart to settle down.

Smoke took the pickup down the street to the light, turned right and drove down the next three streets pointing directly south. Traffic had thinned considerably. There were no lights except for some haze from the few lampposts they'd passed. Other than a couple of stray dogs sniffing through garbage, no one was wandering the streets. This made her feel even more isolated and vulnerable. The nightmare had quickly become unbearably horrifying.

Smoke made another right and they headed southwest, which would take them out of the main section of the city.

Lynn's fears intensified as each road brought them to an even more isolated area. The macadam deteriorated, the weeds grew thick, and the houses built into the side of the rolling hills became less visible.

"We're goin' to the Holler," Smoke said. "We got a great place there."

"It's nice and private." Snickering, Shine had another healthy pull from the bottle.

Lynn continued biting her lip. Scenes from cheap horror flicks spun past, making her even more nauseous.

"Lotta stories 'bout the place." Smoke rubbed her thigh and grinned when she pulled away. "Creepy ones."

Shine chuckled. "We been livin' out here all our lives."

Smoke nodded. "Yup. We bring *all* our lady friends out here."

Lady friends? Was *that* what they called the women they'd kidnapped and brought out here? These two had obviously done this same thing many times before. Her growing fear told her this was something they probably did for fun on their weekends.

Hot stabs of anger quickly rose high above the level of her fear. She had to force herself from lashing out and clawing at their eyes.

"The babes love it out there." Shine leaned against Lynn and moved his whiskey-soaked face closer.

"Eventually," Smoke said.

They both cackled laughter.

Lynn's pulse raced. She clenched her jaw to stifle a scream.

"You'll like it out there, too, baby," Smoke said. "Once we gitcha all warmed up with lotsa home-grown hooch, you'll have yourself a ball."

"Yeah." Shine grinned obscenely. "A *real* ball."

"Been out this way before, baby?" Smoke asked.

Lynn somehow found the courage to shake her head.

"Quiet out here," Smoke said.

"Real quiet." Shine nodded.

"Restful, too."

Shine had more hooch and chuckled. "But not too restful on Friday and Saturday nights, eh, Smoke?"

Smoke barked laughter. Lynn caught a glimpse of two or three missing teeth.

They went down a street and passed several very old, weathered two- and three-story frame houses set into the side of the hill and half-concealed by overgrown grass, bushes, trees and weeds. There were no more streetlamps. Whatever light penetrating the darkness came from the windows of the few distant houses they passed.

The deteriorating two-lane road grew narrower as they continued southwest.

Her blood chilling her to the bone, Lynn couldn't stop thinking about where they were taking her. This area was looking more and more desolate. Even in the harsh beam of the headlights, she couldn't make out anything but hills, trees, wild brush, and tiny flickering lights from the few remote houses far off in the distance. Her heart pounded. She trembled. The nagging dread that she would die out here tonight had grown immensely.

This was all because of Frank. And Ariana.

And because I was too upset and too nonconfrontational to stay there and have it out with them.

She should have stayed right there and told Frank what a selfish, arrogant ass he was. And Ariana needed to know how much their sexual interlude had devastated her older sister. How it had permanently destroyed their relationship. It had clearly demonstrated how much of a cold, self-centered slut Ariana actually was. And it had completely destroyed Lynn's three-year relationship with Frank.

She should have just stood her ground and let it all out while the hurt and the anger were raging through her. Stayed right there with them until she'd stripped them of every single shred of their dignity. And when she'd finished, she should have just gotten back in the Honda and driven back to her apartment. And taken the vodka bottle and gulped down a few. Then gone to bed and considered her future.

But she hadn't. She hadn't because she'd been much too upset to think. And talk coherently. And even manage any sort of reasonable thought processes. The fury going on in her head in that horrible instant had been too much to deal with. For one agonizing moment, she feared that her head would explode.

It had been much simpler to turn her back on them and leave. But in doing so, she'd spared them the humiliation and comeuppance they truly deserved.

And now she was sitting helplessly in a filthy truck with two nasty drunken men who were taking her to their house out in the middle of the boonies, where they planned to get her drunk and do all sorts of nasty things to her.

At the moment, she didn't think she'd ever hated herself more.

If I manage to survive this night...

If I manage to survive any of this...and make it back to St. Clairsville in one piece...

If I can just look the both of them in the eye once more...

Lord, please grant me the opportunity to face them just one more time...

The road narrowed even more and turned bumpier. The gouges and cracks weakening the ancient pavement became crumbling shards of rock and gravel peppering both shoulders. The grass grew taller and wilder just a couple of yards from the road. The few houses extending from the side of the hilly terrain were much less visible.

Before long, there were no further signs of civilization. The decimated, crumbling road dissected into two equally dismal streets leading farther into the fathomless darkness.

Lynn clenched her teeth until her jaw ached. Her hands had become fists so tight that she could no longer feel them. She wanted to scream but feared that the two of them would react violently.

Smoke slowed down at the fork.

Using the truck's headlights as her guide, Lynn scanned the area. Wild brush, trees and tall weeds took over the terrain straight ahead.

Lynn began studying the bottle of whiskey Shine held in his lap. She didn't want to shatter the silence but knew that if she was going to die tonight, it wouldn't hurt to make herself numb before the inevitable happened. For this, she would probably need whiskey to help her. "Could I possibly have a sip…of that…stuff?"

The two stared at her. Shine laughed and handed her the bottle. "Sure, baby. Here. Wet that pucker good."

She took the bottle, flinching at its coolness. Both were silent as they watched her. She wiped off the neck of the bottle, raised it and had a tiny sip.

And nearly choked. The whiskey was so bitter and so strong that she began hacking away.

The two men cackled laughter.

Shine swatted her roughly on the back.

Smoke fired up another cigarette. "Too rich for ya, baby?"

Her eyes were wet and stinging from the strong concoction. And also from Shine's painful swat. She stayed silent for several moments, clearing her tender throat and fighting the anger and the terror that had been building up within her.

"That's from Shine's personal stock," Smoke said. "Sucker makes some strong-ass stuff." Smoke turned to his partner. "Still puttin' in that lighter fluid?"

"Fuckin' A."

Smoke elbowed her. "Gives it that extra kick, don't it?"

Oh my God, she thought, the panic coming back. *I've just swallowed lighter fluid!*

"We don't want piss-water, do we?" Chuckling, Shine took the bottle, had another giant swallow, and handed it back to her.

She stared at it and forced herself to stay strong. Another couple of sips and she'd be so numb, she wouldn't care what they did to her. She could just bide her time and hope she'd get her chance a little later, when they were unconscious from too much of the home-grown hooch. She only hoped she'd be physically able. Her inner sense told her that once they got rough, she might not be able to get away from them.

"Have another swig." Smoke gestured to the bottle.

"Thanks, but I really don't—"

"I *said*, have another *swig*, goddammit."

Lynn sensed genuine rage in the man's venomous tone. It made her flesh crawl. Something in her neck turned cold and began traveling slowly down her spine, making her shudder.

If I don't do as he says, he'd gonna hurt me...

Taking a deep breath, Lynn raised the bottle to her lips. She kept her mouth shut and made it look like she was actually drinking. Her eyes stayed on him as her lips touched the fiery liquid. Then, forcing out a cough, she lowered the bottle and continued hacking away.

Shine laughed and took the bottle.

Smoke slowed down and stopped in the middle of the deserted road. "Our place is down there." His voice had returned to normal as he jabbed a thumb to his right.

About ten yards straight ahead, a break in the tree line went down a steep, brush-covered hill that instantly turned into darkness. Since the truck's headlight beams stopped short, she could see nothing.

This made the nightmare even more terrifying.

"Wh-What's down there?" she asked uneasily.

"Got us a nice little place," Shine said. "Jus' me'n Smoke, Sis, Ma, and her boyfriend Amos."

"And the dogs," Smoke threw in. "Don't forget the dogs."

"'S'right." Shine chuckled. "Two coonhounds, three blue healers and that fuckin' bulldog Hec, sleeps with Ma. Amos don't like ol' Hec in the bed with 'em, but Ma sure does love that Hec. And Ma always gits what she wants."

"Forty acres, most of it fenced." Smoke patted her thigh. "Got us our own still and a nice coupla acres a weed growin' out back, in the apple orchard. Like good homegrown weed, baby?"

Lynn managed a slight nod. She'd only had weed a couple of times, in college. She hadn't liked it very much but didn't want to get them angry. And she sure didn't want to hear Smoke's voice get crazy again.

"Good girl." Shine elbowed her side.

"Kinda tricky, gettin' the pickup down that road." Smoke inched the front of the truck toward the break in the tree line. "Told Amos to make the break wider when he was clearin' things, but that metal plate in his melon he picked up in 'Nam fucked him up for all kindsa memory stuff. Sometimes he still thinks he's back there, fightin' those gooks. A rap or two with the iron skillet usually brings 'im back, but still…" He shrugged.

"We'll make it down," Shine said. "Always do. The Playroom's behind the house. Might as well head there right off." He grinned. "Don't wanna disturb Ma and Amos, do we?"

Lynn nearly gasped. The *Playroom*?

"Got us a nice setup. Used to be an ol' tool shed, but we sorta—"

"Fixed it up," Smoke said with a chuckle.

"Fixed it up *good*," Shine added. "*Real* good. Put in some extra insulation so Ma and Amos don't hear nothin' comin' outa there."

"Got us some nifty gadgets in there." Smoke elbowed her side. "We're gonna have us a ball!"

"Ya won't wanna leave once you're there," Shine said.

"It won't be like you'll be able to—right, Shine?"

The two burst out in wild laughter.

Lynn wanted to stuff her fist into her mouth to stifle the gigantic shriek threatening to tear out of her throat.

I'm not going down there, she promised herself. *I'll do whatever it takes.*

The Playroom. My God…

***

31

Just moments later, her fear subsided.

Something on their left caught her attention just beyond the range of the truck's headlights. At the end of the road, a huge deadfall lay on the ground on the other side of a barbed wire fence. Beyond it, an overgrown field led to a steep hill barely visible behind the column of tall pines.

She had no idea what lay on the other side of the hill. It didn't matter; she had to get out of this truck before they went down that hill. And at the moment, the field quite possibly seemed her best option.

She asked Shine for another sip of the hooch. He handed it over. She gripped it tightly as her thoughts looped, forming the seed of an idea.

"What's that lying in the road?" She pointed to their right.

"Howzat?" Shine stuck his head out the open window. "Don't see nothin'."

"It looked shiny."

The two turned and gawked at her.

She shrugged. "Could be a couple of silver coins. Or maybe jewelry."

Smoke mashed his foot down on the brake. Lynn would have been forced against the dash if she hadn't already braced herself. She watched nervously as Smoke slammed the truck into park and reached for the door.

Shine said, "Lemme look, Smoke. I'm closer."

"We'll *both* look." Smoke pushed his door open.

Shine pulled his head back inside and glanced at Smoke. Frowning, he turned back around and opened the passenger door.

Just as Smoke bent to climb down, Lynn, her pulse pounding wildly, raised the bottle.

And hesitated.

A flurry of images swam past

(Frank and Ariana)

(The Playroom)

(hot and wild)

and in the next instant, blind rage set in, and she slammed him in the back of the head with the bottle. The dull sound went right through her, making her gag. Grunting, Smoke slumped forward. His face thumped into the door frame an instant before he fell roughly to the ground.

Shine spun around to face her.

And in that same instant, she saw Frank grinning at her.

She blinked, and Frank immediately turned back into Shine.

The panic rising inside her, Lynn shoved the heavy base of the bottle into the man's surprised face. Gasping, he fell heavily to the cracked pavement, the back of his head making a dull *clunk*. Moaning, he flopped helplessly on the ground and lay still.

Lynn dropped the bottle on the floor and slid to her right. Below her, Shine was crawling like a dying turtle toward the running board. In just a few seconds, she'd have to step on his hands to jump down. Forcing the panic away, she moved to her left and reached out for the door rest.

Already recovering, Smoke had forced himself up on one knee. He grabbed the running board with his left hand and groped clumsily for her ankle with his right. She pulled away. He reached blindly for her again. Desperate, Lynn brought her foot back down onto the top of the man's head, slamming his forehead into the running board. Moaning, he went back down and lay still.

Lynn had a brief flash of stealing the truck but knew she'd have to run them over to get away. The very idea made her gag. Holding her breath, she prepared to jump out.

Shine, his face swollen and streaked with blood, had already pulled himself up and fumbled for her.

Lynn shifted to her left and jumped down, landing on Smoke's lower back. Wincing at his loud yelp, she dropped onto the macadam, veered around the open door and began running wildly toward the giant deadfall awaiting her at the end of the road.

Chapter 4

It took Lynn only a minute or so to reach the deadfall.

Without looking back, she carefully maneuvered her way through the broken barbed wire. The hazy light coming from the half-moon showed that she was only about ten steps from the deadfall. Without hesitation, she rushed over and plunged directly into it. Even though she could barely see much amongst the broken limbs, she forced herself to keep moving. To get away and gain as much distance as possible. She couldn't let those two find her.

She had no illusions of outsmarting them out here. They were born and raised in this area; they'd know exactly where she was going.

But she didn't want to think about that right now. She wanted only to get away and find some safe place to hide for the night. Her only hope was that in their present state, they'd be more concerned about nursing their wounds and even consider heading back home to sleep it off.

She thought once again of what she'd done and realized she was deluding herself. No one—especially two wild country boys dead-set on a drunken orgy—would let something like that slide.

Get away...

Her inner voice, interrupting her thoughts of fear and hopelessness, urged her to keep moving.

Just moments later, she heard them somewhere behind her, cursing and yelling.

"We're gonna kill ya, bitch!"

"You're dead meat!"

"Damn stupid nasty bitch!"

Get away!

Her inner voice again. She almost smiled when she realized how grateful she was that her subconscious could so easily assume control.

She immediately focused on the most important task ahead—continuing her escape in the penetrating darkness.

The heavy brush grew thicker.

Before she realized it, she could no longer force her way through. She quickly discovered that the brush had completely engulfed her. Panicking, she found that she could no longer budge. She was totally cocooned in heavy weeds and dead limbs and could not see anything in the overwhelming darkness.

Once again, she heard them yelling.

"Bitch!"

"Dead meat!"

"We're gonna find ya!"

Her heart hammering, she burrowed her way deeper into the brush. Just as she did, the angry voices faded away.

It wasn't long before the weeds and limbs enveloping her transformed into comforting warmth. Briefly she considered trying to squirm back out into the open. Exhaustion instantly took over, and she willingly surrendered to the warmth and the safety of her soothing bubble of cool darkness.

With a deep sigh, she closed her eyes and let sleep rock her into a state of relaxed oblivion.

***

Lynn opened her eyes.

Following a moment or two of nervous confusion, she found that her memory had kicked in. Then she recalled what had happened not very long ago. And the two who had brought her out here. And, of course, her escape. And that she was now lying in thick brush on a carpet of dead leaves. Reaching out with both hands to explore the depth of the darkness around her, she pulled back sharply when her palms and forearms raked against stickers, thorns, and exposed branches.

She sat back for a few moments, trying to acclimate her vision. Slices of fresh sunlight peeked at her between the growth and the dead limbs surrounding her. Her heart lifted, and after some careful experimenting, she reached out to clear her way while moving toward the harsh light.

Just beyond the heavy growth, tall weeds took over, and she vaguely remembered the steep hill she'd seen the previous night.

Her heart pumping wildly, she rose on her knees and scanned her surroundings.

The hills were filmed in a golden haze. A forest of pines, intermittent groups of buckeyes and large, half-dead oaks covered the crest.

37

The hazy glare of the morning sun made her shield her eyes. She rubbed them vigorously and waited for them to clear.

Behind her, a huge deadfall lay sprawled amongst the weeds and green moss. It looked like an ancient buckeye that had been struck by lightning and remained standing until the years had weakened it, causing it to disintegrate within and eventually collapse. Its huge torso spanned the length of the path, extending several feet beyond the trees flanking the opening. Judging from the mass of its center, she guessed the trunk to be at least four feet in diameter.

Had she stumbled and fallen while trying to step over it? Or had she tripped on a long piece of jagged limb?

The previous night's events roared back once again. The images of two large, wild-eyed men grabbing her, shoving her into a foul-smelling pickup truck, feeding her homemade whiskey, touching her, rubbing her, swatting her, frightening her half to death...

She tried to remember what else had happened. Their names. Why they'd brought her here.

The answers came back much too quickly.

Shine. Smoke.

They live out here. And they brought me here to take me to their home, where they could do unspeakable things to me in their "Playroom." They fed me whiskey and told me other things, things that should not be remembered...

38

She crawled farther away from the deadfall, stood amongst the weeds and turned back to the overgrown dirt path that proceeded about ten yards straight ahead. To her left, the pines peppering the steep hill pointed toward the sky. She couldn't see beyond them. The hill sloped at a sixty- or seventy-degree angle for maybe a quarter of a mile, then leveled off and turned into another huge mass of woods.

The path straight ahead appeared more promising. Considering her aching body, she didn't want to try such a long, steep climb. And turning around and risking a walk down the road, where she might easily be seen by the two wild guys she'd escaped, presented a very unwise—and dangerous—option.

She decided to examine herself for injuries.

She reached up and gently inspected her head for bumps, cuts and bruises. She was afraid she might have stumbled and knocked it on something during her escape. That could explain the fuzziness.

Despite her fears, she couldn't find any such signs. She examined her fingers, her palms. Turned her hands over and inspected her knuckles and wrists. Her forearms and upper arms were cut and scraped, no doubt by the thorns and dead limbs. She saw very little blood. Just half a dozen or so scratches on each arm. Some dead leaves clung to her hair, some on her shoulders. Her clothes were smudged, dirty and muddy in spots, her jeans ripped near each knee. Nothing big, just some stitching torn loose. The outer edges of her tennis shoes were covered with dirt, but she was reasonably sure she wasn't seriously hurt.

She ran her fingers through her hair to get rid of the dead leaves and twigs. She then gave her shoulders a thorough rub-down. Leaves, dirt, twigs and pine needles dropped quietly to the ground at her feet.

Her self-exam finished, she checked out her surroundings once again and realized that she had no idea where she was. Somewhat uneasy, she tried estimating how long she'd been out here.

Was it just a few hours? Or longer?

The nightmare with Frank and Ariana came back. As a result, Lynn's anger quickly returned. She had the strong feeling that it had never been far away. And that it would always be right there.

Damn you, Ariana. What have you done to me? To us?

How could you destroy what was once a solid relationship over a man who obviously couldn't care about either of us? You've always had your pick of men. You've never had any trouble catching any guy you've ever wanted.

But why Frank?

She knew it would be much better for her if she thought about that later. Much later, when her head had cleared and she no longer had to worry about her safety, or how she was going to get back home.

Right now, her top priority was to figure out what had to be done to get out of this dangerous dilemma.

40

Her thoughts remained cloudy. Strange, indistinct images drifted past, like puffs of smoke. She tried focusing on them but they passed by much too quickly.

Just then, she experienced the strong sensation that she was being followed.

Was the sensation real? Or was her imagination feeding her paranoia?

The panic returning once again, she began moving quickly toward the overgrown dirt path.

Weeds. Tall grass. Thick blankets of pine needles. A trail of pine cones scattered as far as the eye could see. Deadfalls. Gloom everywhere.

You need to get away...

The urge to flee persisted.

She had to stay safe. She just couldn't stay here any longer.

The narrow, weed-choked path beckoned not far away. Pine needles, fallen branches, moss and dead leaves covered the ground. The tall pines hovering above provided a shield from the sun, smothering the path in a thick shroud of darkness.

Despite its foreboding appearance, she hurried toward it and began walking rather briskly. After about a minute, she turned and listened. She paused for only a few seconds before turning back around and continuing her escape. As she moved, her thoughts spun wildly, creating strange, incomprehensible images that made her skin tingle.

Two figures hovered about in the heavy fog clouding her mind. Two men. Both faceless, both dark and cold. A sour reek emanated from them.

41

Feeling the panic again, she shivered, nearly losing her balance.

Stop this.

Use your head—not your imagination.

She had to keep moving. She discovered that the one single sensation sweeping through her at that moment was what urged her to get away.

And with this single horror filling her mind, she bolted toward the narrow dirt road and was once again covered in a heavy cloak of darkness.

Chapter 5

Once Lynn had entered the dark area, the path narrowed even more.

She could barely see her hand in front of her face. The trees grew larger and thicker, their limbs reaching out so far that many had intertwined with one another, making her passage even more difficult.

After another hundred feet or so, the limbs grew shorter and thinner, widening the path between them. The darkness lifted. She could even see the pine needles at her feet. Shards of sunlight flickered as the uppermost branches swayed in the cool morning breeze.

The path abruptly veered to the left. A huge pine tree stood very tall and stately at the curve. The road straightened, remaining this way for thirty or forty yards before dimming once again into heavy darkness.

Just when the darkness of the path grew less dense, she reached a break in the tree line. Where one pine tree should have been, an entrance clearly ten feet wide opened up to a crooked dirt path zigzagging up a steep hill. At its crest, the vague outline of a roof appeared amidst a grove of buckeyes, wild brush, and mighty oaks.

"A witch lives there," said a high-pitched voice behind her.

Cringing, she spun around.

A little boy about eight years old and a small wire-haired dog stood just five feet away, gazing up at her. The boy's face was dirty and smeared with mud. He wore a baggy red tee shirt, jeans two inches too short, and no socks. His scruffy tennis shoes were caked with mud and split open at the sides. The dog's charcoal-gray coat was matted with mud. Panting, it sat on the ground beside the boy, its short, straight tail wagging nervously, swishing aside the pine needles on the ground behind it.

Lynn couldn't help wondering where the two had come from. Since stopping at the foot of the hill, she hadn't seen or heard anything but the chirping of a bird. Estimating the darkness of the road ahead at nearly a hundred yards away, she was totally convinced that there hadn't been enough time for the diminutive twosome to have reached her in so short a time.

She wondered if she was imagining all this.

"Wh-Where'd you two come from?" she asked uneasily.

"We live here," the boy said. He turned to his left and extended a skinny, dirt-covered arm. "Down there, in the Holler." He pointed to another break in the brush, where the short stump of a felled pine tree formed a four-foot gap in the tree line.

The Holler. That was where the two half-drunk maniacs had said they lived.

She wondered for a moment if this boy knew those two. In an isolated setting like this, everyone no doubt knew everyone and everyone's business. This boy's family, for all she knew, could be friends or even relatives of Smoke and Shine. It wouldn't have surprised her one bit if she discovered that this boy lived next door to them.

"You live here with your family?" she asked casually.

He nodded eagerly. "All my life."

She was about to ask how he'd snuck up to her so quickly when the boy suddenly raised his right arm and pointed toward the hill. "Right up there," he said. "At the top of the hill."

"What's up there?"

"The witch." The boy sounded anxious. "She lives there. All alone. In that house."

The boy was obviously joking. Lynn wanted to smile, but his expression remained grim. The boy clearly believed what he'd just told her.

"Really? A *witch* lives there? In a house at the top of that hill?"

The boy nodded. His glum expression had not changed.

"You're sure?"

Another nod.

"Everyone knows there are no witches."

He crossed his arms and looked solemn. "She's really a witch. Everyone says she's a witch."

"But this is the Twenty-First Century. Everyone knows that witches haven't been living here—"

"She's lived there a long—" The boy immediately went silent. He just stared at her, his wide eyes lowering to the ground at her feet, staying there for a few moments before returning to her face. Then he began backing up slowly. His dog's small, pointed ears stood up. The animal jumped up and whined quietly.

"What's wrong?"

The boy's gaze lowered again. His face had paled. He trembled as he studied her. "Wh-What happened to ya? Why are ya all messed up?"

She looked down at herself. And stiffened.

The boy was right. Her jeans were covered with dirt, the slits in them much worse than when she'd initially checked. Dirt covered her tennis shoes, and the cuts on her arms showed prominently from her struggles in the deadfall. She'd seen no blood before but realized that she hadn't been very thorough in her self-examination. Or maybe it was because the shadow of the deadfall had hidden most of her damages from clear view. Right now, in the sunlight, she noticed clotted blood in nearly a dozen places on her hands and wrists.

A thought came to her. She began to wonder if this boy could help her. But first she had to find out if he was related to her two kidnappers. If not, she should have no problem. The boy's family would no doubt have access to a truck or car. Or maybe even an ATV. Out here, you had to have ample transportation. All she had to do was ask him if he could take her back to his home. Maybe his father— or any other available adult—could drive her back to Bridgeport. Or Wheeling if she was lucky. She could offer them gas money, even some extra cash for their troubles. She'd left her handbag under the seat in the Honda but always carried half a dozen twenties in her jeans for emergencies.

46

As long as the boy didn't take her back to her kidnappers, she'd be safe. All she had to do was ask a few innocent questions. It shouldn't be difficult. She knew how to be subtle.

"Listen." She stopped staring at her cuts. "I don't know where I am, so could you please—"

It took her only a moment to realize that she was talking to herself.

The little boy and his dog were gone. They'd obviously vanished while she was taking inventory of her injuries.

Just as she spun around to see where they'd gone, she caught movement to her left, coming from the dark path a hundred yards straight ahead.

Two figures were headed her way.

Two large figures. Moving fast.

A spike of ice shot up her spine.

Was it Smoke and Shine? Could they have already tracked her down?

Or was it someone else?

Didn't matter, did it? She could stay here and find out the hard way—or get out of here while she still had the power to function on her own.

Which way, though? Down the path in the other direction? Or should she attempt to scale the hill that led to the house where the little boy said the witch lived?

Her pulse pounded. In her panic, she could sense her mind threatening to switch off.

Think, Lynn, think!

Which would be her best option?

The path? Or—

The hill obviously provided more seclusion. Trees. Bushes. Tall grass.

The figures were getting dangerously close.

Do something, girl!

Struggling to focus, she darted into the open field and began climbing the steep dirt path that led to the half-hidden structure at the top of the hill.

Chapter 6

Lynn forced herself to keep low and stay as close as possible to anything that might conceal her. She slipped through the tall weeds, moving on all fours as she made her way straight for the trees covering the hill.

Then, just as she crawled past the brush at the foot of one of the tall pines, she heard two loud voices not far behind her.

The fear ripping through her, she stopped cold. Her mind went blank. A flurry of blurred images swept past her vision, and she trembled.

Smoke's bleeding face grinning as he reached for her.

Shine massaging the lump on his head as his thoughts centered on the Playroom.

The two of them tossing her unconscious body in the back of the pickup and easing down the long, bumpy dirt road.

Her world had imploded in a single moment. She forced herself to focus on climbing the hill and hoped this alone would keep the fear from taking over.

She needed to concentrate solely on some way of eluding them. This was the only thing that concerned her at the moment. The only thing that would ensure her getting through the rest of the day alive. She had to forget about Frank and Ariana. They just didn't matter right now.

She had to come up with something tangible. Something that made sense. Something that would shed light on her situation. Now. No matter what else happened, she couldn't let them take her again.

I have to find somewhere to hide. This was her biggest challenge as she trudged through the tall brush.

"We can smell ya, baby!"

They sounded like they were only fifty feet or so behind her.

"I don't like gettin' this close," one of them muttered.

"Don't be a pussy," barked the other.

What were they talking about?

The footsteps continued.

"We're gonna getcha, bitch!"

More giggling, growing louder.

In less than a minute, they'd be able to tell exactly where she was.

"We're kinda pissed atcha for wastin' that good homegrown hooch on our heads…"

"Twasn't very neighborly, baby…"

Her pulse racing, she ducked down deeper into the weeds. When she heard their footsteps getting closer, she veered off the dirt path and crawled into a nest of heavy brush. A large gouge in the ground enabled her to conceal herself deeper into the earth. Taking a deep breath, she curled up, fetus-like, and lay very still, hoping the heavy thumping of her heart wouldn't give her away.

The footsteps sounded closer as they ascended the hill.

"Where'd ya go, baby?"

"We know you're up here."

The footsteps stopped abruptly.

"We know you're here…"

"We're gonna be awfully pissed off if ya don't c'mon out…"

"Pissed and horny, baby. Pissed and horny."

A brief silence.

"Where the fuck *is* she?"

"She went right up here. She's gotta be hidin' out there in the grass somewhere."

"Up *there*?"

More silence.

"Her *house*?"

A pause. "Think she'd go…*there*?"

"If she's scared enough…"

"That's right. She ain't no local. She…don't know about…about her…"

"That's why she went up there, moron."

More silence.

"Smoke?"

"I know, I know…"

"We *can't* go up there. Not up *there*… No fuckin' way. We both know we don't wanna get anywhere *near* that place."

"I know, man. I know."

"But if *she's* up there…"

"She ain't there, dammit. How many times do I gotta—"

"Some say she's still up there. Some say she'll always be."

"Like I told ya a zillion times before, that don't make no sense."

"Even if she ain't there no more, her voodoo's still there. In that house. Can't ya feel it?"

"I still ain't sure about that—"

"It don't matter, man. Why d'ya think we keep hearin' so many weird stories about it? We been hearin' that shit since we were little. We ain't goin' up there. *I* sure as hell ain't!"

The sound of a door creaking open.

Heavy footsteps on a hollow wooden floor.

Silence.

Then, a harsh whisper: "H-hear that, Smoke?"

"I'm standin' right here beside ya, moron. Goddamn right I heard it."

"Think it's—"

"Can't be…"

"Then who d'ya think—"

"Ain't nobody s'posed to be livin' there, goddammit… No one's been livin' there since we were little shits."

"Heard Amos say somethin' the other day, said he saw some dude in a fancy ride sittin' at the bottom of the hill on the back road, takin' pitchers."

"Was Amos hittin' the hooch when he said it?"

"Never can tell. That plate in his head messes 'im up all the time."

"Messes 'im up less when he's hittin' the hooch."

"Still don't know about this…"

"Why'd anyone wanna take pitchers?"

"No idea."

"Then who d'ya think's standin' there on that porch?"

A pause. "Can't see from here. Weeds and scrubs and that goddamn pine tree in the way. I don't wanna get no closer. Do *you*?"

"Could be her, Smoke…"

"Don't care what the hell they say, she *ain't there*."

"Then who—"

"Don't wanna stay here and find out."

Scrambling.

The frenzied footsteps rapidly grew distant. In just moments, they disappeared.

Dead silence.

Her heart still pounding, Lynn waited for more of the blessed silence.

Less than ten seconds later, the door of the house slammed shut.

The heavy silence resumed.

***

Too terrified to move, Lynn lay fetus-like in her cocoon of concealment.

But even in her anxious state she couldn't stop wondering about her next move. Should she leave her tiny sanctuary and face whoever was living in the house? Unless she was mistaken, she was almost certain that whoever had come out onto the porch was no friend of Smoke or Shine. Otherwise, she would have been faced with *three* stalkers, and a horror much worse than her present one.

"A witch lives there."

"Some say she's still up there. Some say she'll always be."

The boy had said it, and both Smoke and Shine obviously believed it. Why else had they scrambled back down the hill the moment they'd heard someone opening the front door?

What in heaven's name would frighten two rough, half-drunk country boys so easily?

Was there actually a witch living in that house?

She thought about that and quickly realized that it didn't matter. What mattered was that whoever was living there had scared away her abductors.

Taking a deep breath, Lynn crawled out of her concealment and sat out in the open, gazing down the hill.

No sign of anyone. Which was a good thing.

She turned back to the house.

Except for an ancient glider and a few weathered boards, the front porch was empty. Whoever had scared away the twosome had apparently gone right back inside.

Her imagination kicked in again, her mind buzzing with disturbing images from *Texas Chainsaw Massacre*, *The Hills Have Eyes*, and other equally creepy flicks.

Stop this and get a grip!

Focusing on more pertinent matters, Lynn continued studying the house.

A two-and-a-half-story frame dwelling, its front walls were weather-beaten, its steep roof covered with pine needles that had fallen from the pines towering above it. The front porch appeared just as battered as the house, its broken lattices pulled apart and crumbling, its front steps cracked and broken, deteriorated by the elements over a period of many years. The two front windows had obviously once been boarded up. Some of the boards had loosened and lay on the porch or hung by a nail. The wooden rail needed major maintenance. One of the springs supporting the glider had broken. Its seat rested at an angle on the wooden floor.

The place was probably pretty and warm at one time, its inhabitants friendly and happy. Although it now had the look of a haunted house, it just didn't give her that feeling. And as she continued gazing at it, she sensed a growing warmth and affection.

She suddenly realized that she'd stopped worrying about the two hunting her.

Ignoring the stiffness in her muscles and joints, she pulled herself to her feet. Another quick glance down the hill revealed no movement or any activity amongst the wild brush. Relieved, she turned and walked up to the house, then carefully ascended the three wobbly front steps. After a few moments of tense hesitation, she knocked on the door.

There was no answer.

Resisting the urge to turn around and walk back down the hill, she knocked again.

Silence.

She remembered something else one of them had said.

"Ain't nobody s'posed to be livin' there…"

A moment later, something else nudged her memory: *"No one's been livin' there since we were little shits."*

It did indeed look abandoned. In fact, it had the appearance of a house that hadn't been occupied for many years.

But the door had opened. She'd heard it. Smoke and Shine had heard it as well. And, judging by their reaction, someone had actually opened it and come outside. And stood on the front porch.

Who had they seen?

They hadn't seen anything. Judging by what she'd heard them say, weeds, scrubs, and a pine tree had obscured their view.

But it didn't matter. Whatever happened had scared them enough to send them scurrying back down the hill.

Who—or what—could scare those two away so easily?

Was it a witch?

Lynn realized right then that she had two options. The first one was simple. She should turn around and climb back down the hill. And face whatever horror awaited her at the bottom of the hill. The two looking for her might be lying in wait behind a bush, more than eager to pounce on her the moment they saw her.

Option Two faced her only a few inches away.

The door.

Open it. Forget all about what happened before.

She had no idea what awaited her on the other side of the door. A witch? Something worse? Something frightening enough to scare away two rough, half-drunk country boys with vengeance in their minds?

She could think of no other option. And as she gazed numbly at the large weathered wooden door, she knew she had nothing to lose. And now it was time to make a decision. She could either stand here like an idiot until she collapsed from exhaustion, fear, or starvation, or she could handle this in a mature sort of way. All she had to do was stand tall and strong and face whatever was lurking beyond the door. And if it meant her death, then so be it.

She just didn't want to climb back down that hill and face those two again.

Taking a deep breath, she moved one step closer, reached out and tested the ancient glass doorknob.

A spark jumped from it, making her cringe and pull back.

What on earth?

Silly girl. This is nothing more than static electricity. You've been to high school and college. You should know all about stuff like that.

Her arm trembled the moment she reached for it again. After several more half-hearted attempts, her fingers made contact with it again.

No sparks this time.

Somewhat more confident, she closed her hand around it, wincing at its coldness, its roughness.

The knob wobbled, turning easily.

Her pulse thumping erratically, Lynn took a breath and gently pushed open the door.

The foyer was dark and empty. An ancient chandelier hung from the high ceiling, long, slender cobwebs dangling from it. A strong mixture of mildew and disinfectant hung in the air.

There was a door on her left. It was also closed.

She gazed uneasily at it, wondering if she should open it.

For the next several minutes, she stood stock-still, staring fearfully at it, her mind feverishly working on creating some sort of monster awaiting her on the other side.

Monster? Or witch?

Or was the room empty?

You'll never know as long as you stand here like an idiot, wondering...

Just then, she heard footsteps descending the stairs behind her.

Her heart skipped a beat. She spun around.

And glimpsed a large shadow descending the stairs.

The events of the last few hours suddenly caught up to her, and she blacked out.

Chapter 7

Darkness.

Warmth.

The darkness finally lifted.

A tall, slender woman with long, flowing red hair, a sharp-featured face and large deep-blue eyes appeared. She stood facing Lynn just a few feet away, her white chiffon dress embellished with bright blue sequins twinkling in the dark room.

"Are you all right, child?" the woman asked in a soft, low-pitched voice.

"I *think* so..." Everything seemed cloudy, disjointed. Was this a dream? Lynn had the strong feeling that it wasn't. She could tell she was awake. And this was real. "What happened? Did I pass out?"

"Yes, child. You've had a very rough night."

Her memory instantly started up. Yes. It had been much worse than rough. The two who had forced her into their truck and brought her out here. Their stench, their foulness. Their horrible closeness.

The image of the whiskey bottle flashed brightly. One of them handing it to her. Lynn cringing at its disgusting taste. Then, slamming them both in the head with the heavy bottle. Jumping out of the truck. Escaping, running away...

And, finally, struggling to climb a steep, brush-covered hill.

Where was she? What place was this?

Who was this beautiful lady?

The unfamiliar room was cold-looking. A heavy scent of mildew clung to the air. A night table stood next to the bed. An ancient-looking rocker sat in the far corner, just a couple of feet from a boarded-up window.

As her head cleared, she remembered a large, abandoned house sitting at the very top of the grass-covered hill. And a front porch. And a front door with a glass doorknob. And a high-ceilinged foyer with a long staircase and an ancient chandelier covered with a heavy cloak of dust and cobwebs.

She'd opened a door. And then—

Footsteps? A shadow?

Then she'd fainted—

Or *had* she?

What else could have happened?

How in heaven's name did she get into this bed?

And why was everything so dark? So shadowy? Why did it seem like all this had happened so long ago?

"Are you all right, my dear?" the beautiful red-headed woman asked again.

"Well…I'm not really sure. I don't think I can really be sure about anything right now. My head…" She reached up and gingerly touched the back of her skull.

"As I just said, you've had a rough night. And you did pass out."

"I guess I must have." Something occurred to her. "Who are you? And where am I?"

The woman smiled, displaying small dimples on each side of her mouth. The room quickly seemed very warm and bright when she smiled. Lynn couldn't help thinking how much better she suddenly felt. It was almost like everything bad that had happened the night before dimmed in the woman's brightness, vanishing an instant later.

"You don't remember anything?" the lady asked.

"I don't remember much at all." She rubbed her eyes. "Not after I came in through the front door." More images drifted back in cloudy waves.

The two drunken men following her.

The hill.

The little boy and his dog. "*A witch lives there.*"

The house.

"*Some say she's still up there.*"

My God. I'm in her house!

Suddenly alert, she scanned her surroundings.

The room revealed nothing.

The lady continued smiling at her. Smiling, waiting for Lynn to speak.

"Who *are* you? Are you…I mean…do you…Do you live here?"

The woman's smile remained.

Moments later, she began fading.

A soft tapping at the door made Lynn's pulse sputter.

Silence.

About half a minute later, the knob turned, and the door slowly creaked open…

A figure appeared in shadow and stood quite still for several moments before taking a single step into the room. When the shadow ended, the figure's features became clearer.

It was a tall, slender man.

Lynn forced herself not to panic. To wait and see what was going to happen. After all, this man didn't have a weapon in his hands. He wasn't moving very quickly and he certainly didn't look menacing.

But even so, she couldn't help wondering what was going on. Where had the beautiful red-haired lady gone? And how was it possible that she'd vanished into thin air the moment this man knocked on the door?

Was the lady real?

She had to be. She'd spoken, hadn't she? She'd smiled, asked questions. She was very pleasant and genuinely concerned about how Lynn was feeling.

But the moment this man had knocked on the door, the lady disappeared.

Who was this man? Judging by what happened outside, she was almost certain that he was no friend of the two who had brought her out here. But this didn't tell her anything about him. Nor did it explain his intentions.

Very quickly she took inventory of her situation. For one thing, she wasn't tied to the bed. And she was covered with a large, musty-smelling afghan. Those were good signs, weren't they? They suggested consideration. Kindness. It also suggested that she was not a kidnap victim.

Something else occurred to her. Something that suddenly made her uneasy. And frightened.

With trembling hands, she grasped the end of the afghan and pulled it up. And sighed in relief.

She was still wearing her clothes.

This was also good, right? Yes. In fact, it was great. It convinced her that she hadn't been brought up here by a degenerate.

So why did she still feel vulnerable?

The man took another step closer to the bed.

Lynn felt her entire body cringing.

The man obviously sensed her fear. "I have absolutely no intention of doing you any harm. You fainted downstairs, so I just carried you up here, put you in the bed and covered you with the afghan. Sorry it's so old and funky. It was the first thing I could find. I haven't had the chance to wash it yet."

She immediately felt silly.

The more she heard the man's voice, the less frightened she felt. It was a quiet, gentle voice and made her feel less tense. Less afraid.

She managed a timid smile. "I'm sorry. I just—"

"I understand."

"It's been a long night for me."

"I guess you were the one those two were looking for. Out in the front yard?"

She nodded. "I'm sure glad they decided to give up."

He didn't reply.

Her curiosity flared up. "Any reason why they did?"

63

He shrugged. "This house seems to be off-limits to the locals."

"So I've heard." She waited for him to elaborate, but he didn't.

After a moment, he smiled. "Hungry?"

She suddenly realized how long it had been since she'd last eaten. At that same moment, she heard her stomach reply in protest. "Yes. I am, actually…"

The light coming in from the hall shone on him. He was a nice-looking man around forty with short, professionally styled dark hair and fine features. He was clean-shaven. There was a softness in his light-gray eyes that made her feel even worse for prejudging him.

He was wearing a cream-colored dress shirt and black slacks. His sleeves were rolled up, exposing a gold watch and two pale, slender forearms. It made her wonder if he worked in a bank, or office. She immediately thought of one of those guys in an insurance commercial, or an actor plugging the latest software.

I'm losing my mind, she thought. *I'm lying in a strange bed in a strange house and thinking about a stupid TV commercial, because a nice-looking man is standing at the foot of the bed, asking me if I'm hungry…*

I really need to stop thinking nonsense.

This made her realize that she had to find out a few important things.

"H-How did I get here?"

64

"I found you out in the foyer. As I just said, you'd passed out, so I brought you up here. You obviously needed some rest. You looked all done in. I can't help wondering if you were hiding in the bushes all night."

"I have."

"I figured as much. But anyway, I guessed you wouldn't mind resting in a regular bed for a change."

"Really? Honestly?" Something about this just didn't make any sense.

He shrugged and gave her a sort of half-smile. "I thought that would be much better than stepping over you all day."

She liked his smile but forced herself to stick to more urgent matters. And this meant trying to determine what was really going on. "Why didn't you call the police? I *was* trespassing, you know…"

"You were also trying to get away from the Pozners."

"*That's* their name?"

"I saw them in the living room window when they were halfway up. I think they're half-brothers—if that makes any difference. One's dark and the other's blonde, and they both wear leather and don't seem to care about bathing much. I've heard a slew of stories about that brood. They've got some sort of a pot grow in their back yard, about two miles down the road. Sometimes you can smell it if the wind's blowing up the hill."

"That sounds like them."

"I figured I ought to give you a break. As I just said, I've heard so many stories about them. I don't know which to believe and which to dismiss, but what little I've seen about them tells me that their family isn't what you could call nice. Or even civilized. They're strictly right out of *Deliverance*."

"I agree."

He pointed to her left, toward the doorway. "The bathroom's out there. The first door on your left, down the hall. I laid out some fresh towels. C'mon down when you're ready. I'm fixing bacon, scrambled eggs, and toast. And coffee."

His suggestion was like music to her ears. She had to force herself to keep from salivating.

"I'll be right down," she said.

He smiled. Then he turned, left the room and closed the door softly behind him.

Lynn swung her legs over the side of the bed and sat there, letting her body gradually acclimate itself to the shifted position. A few minutes later, just as she got up and took a few steps toward the door, a low-pitched voice behind her whispered, "Be careful, my dear. Don't be taken in by him. He's not a believer."

She turned around sharply.

No one was there.

Chapter 8

The succulent smells of freshly brewed coffee and crispy bacon drifted up from the first floor as Lynn descended the stairs.

Although still shaken by everything that had happened in the last twelve hours, Lynn wanted to concentrate on breakfast. And a few other things, as well.

The item heading the list was, of course, the Honda. She had to get back to Wheeling and pick it up before it was towed away and impounded. Then, once she returned to St. Clairsville, she faced the extremely unpleasant task of deciding how to deal with Frank and Ariana. She obviously could never trust him again. Any man who would have sex with his girlfriend's sister was not someone any girl with an acceptable number of working brain cells would choose to share her life with. The fact that Ariana was merely twenty-three would explain her immaturity and recklessness. It might also excuse her foolish motivations. And the fact that Frank was a successful businessman well-known in the Ohio Valley would make him even more irresistible for someone of Ariana's age and emotional instability.

However, nothing could explain what Frank had done.

The mixed aromas of coffee and bacon grew increasingly enticing as she reached the bottom of the staircase. Her mind now focused solely on breakfast, Lynn tossed all other unpleasant thoughts aside.

***

Ancient furniture filled the large, bright room.

Cobwebs bobbed lazily from the corners of the high ceilings, but most of the furniture was free of dust and recently polished. The large oval-shaped Turkish rug covering the floor had recently been cleaned. The glittering sunlight filtering in through the drapes splashed a layer of gold on the surface of the dining room table.

The man in the dress shirt carefully placed a large plate of scrambled eggs and bacon onto the center of the table. He looked up at her and smiled. "Please. Have a seat." He gestured to the chair opposite him. Then he turned and hurried through the wide archway at the other end of the room, which no doubt led to the kitchen.

Lynn sat down and stared longingly at the plate of food. She wanted to dig right in but didn't want to be rude. It was all she could do to pull her eyes away from the delicious-looking display and hoped she wouldn't have to wait too long to enjoy her breakfast.

Moments later, he came back carrying a plate heaped with sliced buttered toast. He set it on the table. "Please help yourself."

"*Thank* you." She grabbed a large spoon and dropped a heaping helping of scrambled egg onto her plate, then picked up four strips of crispy bacon and a slice of toast. "Hope you don't mind my fingers, but I'm *starving*."

"Not at all." He sat down facing her. "Coffee?"

"That would be *heavenly*."

He picked up the coffeepot and poured some steaming black coffee into her cup, then his own.

She munched on a piece of delicious bacon and tried not to embarrass herself. It tasted wonderful, and she wanted to offer this man her soul for providing such a wonderful feast. But she forced herself to stick to matters that wouldn't suggest that she might be crazy. "You live here alone?"

"Not exactly." He helped himself to some eggs, bacon and two pieces of toast. "I'm sorry, but I didn't introduce myself earlier. I'm Bryan. Bryan Grant."

"Lynn Monroe." She swallowed a forkful of delicious egg and immediately felt her energy level rising. "By the way, Bryan Grant, you're a terrific cook."

He laughed. "You *must* be starving."

"Even if I am, you're still a great cook."

He had a sip of coffee. "I guess now you can tell me what you were doing out there this morning. And why those Pozner idiots were after you."

Smiling sheepishly, she nibbled on a piece of toast and wondered what she should say. She could tell by how he'd been treating her that he was an okay guy. And since he'd carried her upstairs, laid her down in bed and covered her with an afghan instead of trying anything funny, or having her arrested for trespassing, she decided to tell him the truth. "It's very simple. They picked me up in Wheeling and wanted to take me back to their place and do all sorts of nasty things to me. I managed to get away from them by hiding in the bushes in the grove out front. That's how I got my clothes so filthy dirty. It's how I got cut up, too."

"Did you want to get the local cops involved?"

"Not really…"

He tilted his head. "We *are* talking kidnapping, aren't we?"

"Well, since I got away from them and don't want to have to worry about them finding me again if something weird or unexpected happens during a trial…" She just shrugged.

He had another forkful of egg and some toast, then washed it down with more coffee. "Sounds reasonable to me."

"Really?"

"You definitely raise a good point. Judging by what I've heard about those two, I wouldn't put anything past them. They're not exactly what you could call cultured."

"I don't know *what* I'd call them."

"They're dangerous. Everyone around here knows that. They like to get roaring drunk and act like something right out of a horror flick. You're extremely lucky you were able to get away from them."

"I'm really surprised they didn't try looking harder for me. I wouldn't think that grove I found just down the hill would actually keep them from looking."

"No one likes coming up here."

She tried a gamble. "Because of the witch?"

70

He stopped eating. "They actually *mentioned* her?" Before she could respond, he shrugged. "They would. Everyone around here stays clear of this place."

"A little boy mentioned her, too."

He blinked. "A little boy?"

"He had a little dog with him. A gray wired-haired dog. It looked like it probably weighed no more than five pounds. Possibly a terrier mix. Both of them were filthy dirty. They obviously spend a lot of time in the woods."

Bryan sat in silence, looking pensive. Then, after another sip of coffee, he said, "Can't say that I've seen them. In fact, I haven't seen a little boy living out here at all. But I haven't really seen everyone, mind you. Just people I happen to run across while I'm doing errands in town. The Pozners are quite possibly the youngest males I've seen living out here, and they're both in their mid-thirties. Everyone else is either retired or just a handful of years from retirement. The younger crowd works in Bridgeport, or Wheeling. Most of the men work at the machine shops, or at the wharf. The ones with education and ambition left the area years ago."

"I guess you just never ran across the little boy."

"As you just said, he probably plays in the woods all the time."

"He told me he's been living out here all his life."

71

"Well, I don't actually live out here, so I can't really say too much at all about the locals."

She found this very odd. It made her wonder what he was doing here. "You...don't live here?"

"I'm just staying here to sell the house."

"Your family owns this place?"

"My relatives lived here for a very long time. As I've been told, they moved here in the mid-fifties or early sixties. When my aunt died two months ago, there were no other relatives, so I inherited this place. I came here a couple of weeks ago to get everything in order so I can sell it."

As he was talking, Lynn caught something out of the corner of her eye. Something in white. A slender figure with flowing red hair.

Just as she turned, she found that she was staring at her own reflection in the glass doors of the massive china cabinet on the opposite wall.

"Something wrong?" he asked.

She stiffened. "W-Why do you ask?"

"You looked kind of...well, spooked."

She smiled sheepishly. "I think it was just the way the sun reflected in the china cabinet. It...kind of startled me." She forced herself to gaze at the man and forget about what she imagined she'd just seen. It wasn't difficult at all. Bryan was fairly easy on the eyes—it didn't take much of an effort to stay focused on him.

Anyway, ignoring what she thought she'd seen made good sense. She didn't want to ask him if he thought the ghost of a beautiful redheaded woman was haunting this house. She didn't want to upset him and, as a result, ruin this delightful breakfast. And she certainly didn't want him to think she might be a fruitcake.

He smiled. "This place has that effect on people."

"It's not haunted, is it?"

"I don't think so. I haven't actually seen or experienced any solid evidence of it…"

"Local lore, I guess."

"In a remote area like this, spooky stories tend to fly around and survive throughout generations. Since most of the people here are superstitious to begin with, weird stuff feeds the stories floating around, keeping them alive. But I really can't blame anyone living out here. I've only been staying here a couple of weeks, but even though I'm not what you'd call superstitious, I must admit that this place tends to get creepy. Especially in the evenings."

"Why?"

"I think it's the isolation. The wind adds to it, especially at night. The wind—and of course, the creaking of the building settling on its foundation. I've been out in the back yard at night, and when the wind drifts through the trees a certain way, it sounds an awful lot like whispering." He smiled sheepishly. "I'm not ashamed to say that it—well, it unnerved me."

"But you generally don't believe in any of that spooky stuff, then?"

"As I just said, I never was superstitious. I can't speak for my relatives, but…" He smiled sheepishly.

73

"Then you're here just to sell the house?"

"And the moment I get the papers, I'm gone. I'm trying really hard to make a quick sale in a couple of weeks. I don't know if I can do it, so I've decided to drop the price substantially if someone expresses an interest. The appraisal I've just had done on the property might help quite a bit."

"Where do you live?"

"I've been a Pittsburgher the last thirty years. I grew up in Wheeling, but my folks moved to the Tristate area when I was about nine. I've been living in Fox Chapel the past fifteen years, but I work in Pittsburgh. I run my own insurance company."

"And you say you've been here two weeks?"

"Twelve days, to be precise, and even that seems too long. Apparently I can't get anyone interested."

"Because everyone thinks it's haunted?"

"I know this whole haunted house idea is silly, but when you're dealing with the general public, you've got to expect silliness. And every conceivable form of stupidity."

"But how do you know about any of this stuff? Have you been asking around? Or have you had the chance to talk to any of the locals?"

"As an insurance salesman, I've always had to be a good researcher. Selling a house is no different from studying and working on policies. Since I've been here, I've done some serious work on the history of this place. I've learned some very strange things about it."

"Like what?"

He paused before he spoke again. "The house may not be haunted, but many locals over the years have come to the conclusion that it's enchanted."

She just stared at him.

"There's a difference, you know."

"Haunted—that's sort of the opposite of enchanted, isn't it? The way I've heard it, it's the difference between white and black—am I right?"

"That's actually a very polite, generic definition of it."

"So then...how would this place be enchanted?"

"Well, judging by what I've learned from my relatives and from many of the locals I've talked to, somewhere down the line, one of my ancestors was known to be a witch."

Chapter 9

A witch lives there…

Lynn felt a strange tingling moving up her spine.

"Her name was Margaret Freedman." Bryan seemed to be staring off into space. "And going by everything I've heard about her, she was apparently known as a white witch."

Lynn's thoughts centered on the beautiful redhead she'd seen upstairs when she'd first awakened. And standing in front of the china cabinet just moments ago.

And, of course, the voice she'd heard just before leaving the bedroom.

The image of the woman's striking, sharp-featured face filled her mind. Her beautiful smile. The large, sparkling deep-blue eyes. The luxurious, flowing red hair…

Her wonderful brightness. Her warmth.

Was it the spirit of Margaret Freedman that had appeared to her? If so, why had she shown herself? What did she want?

It didn't matter, did it? At least, not now. The important thing was that Lynn shouldn't reveal anything right now. Bryan was watching her—possibly looking for some sort of reaction.

Her inner sense suggested that she not tell him anything. That things would go much better for both of them if she didn't tell him what she'd seen.

After all, didn't the spirit tell her to be careful?

He's not a believer...

She drank some coffee and was pleased that her nerves had finally settled down. "You said a *white* witch, didn't you? That's...that's a *good* thing...isn't it?"

"I haven't done much research on it, I'm afraid. Not as much as I'd like. I'm much too busy trying to run my Smithfield Street office remotely while scheduling appointments for this property with the local realtor, who has his office in Wheeling. But yes. According to the locals, Margaret was good, and very well-liked, as well. Home remedies, chants, spells—the whole nine yards. We're talking more than a hundred years ago, mind you. But these locals are strange. It's like they're still living in the last century. They've got all the latest toys and gimmicks everyone else has these days— computers, iPads, notebooks, cellphones, the Net— but they're still locked into an era reminiscent of the fifties or sixties. You can't shake the strong feeling that they haven't accepted the New Millennium."

"There are a lot of people like that," she said. "Especially those living in remote areas."

"Well, I'm afraid this one's no different."

"That's the feeling I'm getting. Especially since what those two said about their home while they were taking me there."

He smiled. "The Pozner boys were born and raised out here, but you shouldn't think everyone else out here is anything like them. The Pozners aren't typical. I kind of think there was some inbreeding involved with that brood. The others?

77

They're country people, but they're mostly quiet and shy, and keep to themselves."

"But not dangerous?"

"Generally, no. The Pozners apparently have been a problem since they were children. Fighting in school. Vandalism. Truancy. And they both have records as adults."

"Why am I not surprised?"

"From what I've learned, it's mostly small-time stuff. Malicious mischief. Drunk and disorderly. Liquor store theft. Some drugs, but not the heavy stuff. Weed and glue-sniffing when they were in high school, some cocaine…"

"No rape charges?"

"I didn't see anything about that, but it wouldn't surprise me one bit if they'd done a felony or two and gotten away with it. Not much law enforcement out here, apparently."

"Would *you* want to come out here if you were a cop?"

"Only if I absolutely had to." He picked up a strip of bacon. "You never did tell me where you're from."

"St. Clairsville."

"And the Pozners picked you up in Wheeling?"

"Just scooped me right off the street and tossed me in their pickup."

He frowned. "I knew it had to have been something like that. It's really none of my business, of course, but I just couldn't see a connection—or any sort of attraction—between you and them."

"It's a long story. Please don't ask me to tell you why I was in Wheeling in the first place."

"As I just said, it's none of my business."

Relieved, she decided it was time to get back to the important subject. "So then, you really don't believe in any of that stuff? Witchcraft? Black magic? Or, as in your ancestor's case, white magic?"

"I'm much too preoccupied with life and its complications, paying my bills and running my business. I don't have the time or the inclination to bother with anything else. To me, stuff like that is nothing more than an unnecessary distraction. Superstition never really came into my life. Not even when I was a child. I guess you could call me a hard-facts kind of guy."

He's not a believer...

Once again, the beautiful redhead's words invaded her thoughts.

"Don't tell me *you* do?" he asked suddenly.

"I honestly don't know what I believe. But while we're on the subject...why would you say this place is enchanted?"

"That's another story entirely. And, as you might have already guessed, it also involves Margaret Freedman."

"Please tell me about it."

"Well, as I've already said, the lady Margaret Freedman was known in these parts as a good witch. Her words, apparently. And many locals believed she was. She lived here almost her entire

79

life—which, I understand, was nearly a hundred years."

"If she was a good witch, why is everyone in this area so afraid of this place?"

"These people living here now are not really interested in the fact that Margaret was a good witch. The fact that she was a witch, period, was more than enough to get their attention. And, of course, to get them to stay clear."

"Was she ever married?"

He shook his head. "I've never been able to find out. I know how strange that sounds, coming from a distant relative—especially one who's done some research on the family. But that's the honest truth. Apparently, no one ever saw anyone else living here with her. Other than the hired help, that is. She preferred living by herself and devoting her life to practicing her craft and helping people. And from what I've heard, she was extremely popular. Whenever one of the locals took sick, they went straight to Margaret and asked her to look in on them and do whatever she could, using her special talents to heal or help whoever needed some sort of miracle."

"Did she ever heal anyone?"

"From what I've learned, she helped just about everyone who asked for her assistance."

"This must have infuriated the local doctors."

"Back then, things were much different, of course. Very isolated. This was long before TV, and radio was merely in its infancy. In other words, word of mouth served as everyone's main source of

80

communication. The locals knew Margaret was very special, so they didn't want to do anything that would spoil the status quo. They also knew that if anyone else found out about her, there would be an inquiry. The authorities would swoop in and put an end to everything. Folks were even more laid back in those days than they are now, but doctors still turned radical whenever talk of an unorthodox healer came up."

"Even so, I imagine she earned quite a reputation."

"But it didn't stop there. The word eventually got out, and it wasn't long before other sorts of people began making the trip to the house."

"*Other* sorts?"

"Couples who wanted to get married. Locals who were in love and wanted to spend their lives together. There were also those with mental problems who wanted to see her so she could help them."

"Did she?"

"From what I've heard, yes."

Lynn wondered how much of this woman's story was true and how much was local folklore. She knew all about legends and superstitions and gossip. She also knew how local tales grew unbelievable and turned more and more bizarre with each retelling over the years.

But she had to consider the obvious. She'd seen the spirit of a beautiful woman who quite possibly could be the lady Bryan Grant was talking about.

And she'd spoken to Lynn.

Yes. That was the clincher. She'd not only *appeared* to her, but she'd also *spoken*. And no matter what Lynn did or did not believe, she couldn't deny what she'd seen and heard the moment she'd entered this house.

Even so, some of the things Bryan had told her just didn't make sense.

"I don't think I quite understand. How would this lady be able to help people with mental problems?"

"This is where my skepticism comes into play," Bryan said. "I don't believe a word about any of this legend stuff."

"None of it?"

He thought for a moment before responding. "Margaret Freedman indeed existed. That much is evident in the old family albums I've stumbled across over the years. I also believe she lived in this house. I can also accept the fact that she helped people. Home remedies, midwifing—things like that. And I can quite possibly manage to come to grips with the fact that this woman practiced some sort of witchcraft. But as far as actually *healing* people?" He shook his head. "Sorry, but I just can't wrap my modern mind around that one."

"Did she have medicines? Herbs? Potions? Does any of this involve Voodoo? Or am I looking at this all wrong?"

"Judging by what I've heard, Margaret Freedman kept a room upstairs where she took people for their sessions."

"Upstairs?"

82

"Across the hall from the room where you were sleeping, as a matter of fact."

"That was where she practiced her witchcraft? Or whatever she did to help people?"

"Yes."

She sensed her curiosity rising again. "Is there anything in there now? Or has it been cleaned out?"

"As far as I can tell, it's just a regular bedroom. Nothing else in there that I'd consider strange. Or even remotely unusual."

"Nothing?"

He thought about that for a moment. "Since you asked, something about that room does seem a tad strange."

"Strange how?"

"Nothing supernatural or creepy, as you might think. I guess depressing would be a more suitable term."

"Depressing?"

"I'd say it's most likely the stale air. Possibly because the windows have been painted shut, and it's literally impossible to open them. I've had the cleaning crew come in several times to air out all the rooms, but that particular one..." He shook his head.

"Maybe the windows should be replaced."

"I don't really want to spend a lot of money on this place. I'd just like to sell it at a low price and be on my merry way."

"I understand."

"But getting back to that room...There's certainly nothing in the air—nothing magical, that is—floating around in there."

"Maybe she cleaned it out herself before she died. She might have decided that she was getting too old to continue working her magic and should get rid of everything."

"I have no idea. From what I've learned about her, she was a very secretive lady. No one ever knew what she was up to."

"Well, she apparently brought people into that room and did strange things that helped many of them in some way."

"All I've heard was that the locals considered it a place where her patients went to cleanse themselves."

"Spiritually?"

"Possibly. I've also heard that couples who wanted to stay in love forever would follow her into that room, where she'd perform a spell to make sure they'd remain in love with one another no matter what else happened in the course of their lives. And that people who thought they were inhabited by demons would voluntarily go in that room with her to be exorcised."

"Now that sounds seriously scary."

Bryan nodded. "The whole concept creeps me out. Especially that exorcism part."

"I can't say as I blame you. And now you're staying here and sleeping upstairs. Are you having any trouble getting through the night?"

84

"I don't scare easily. Believe me, I've been in that special room of hers several times. I've had quite a few problems with local cleaning services, but I recently found a good one from Wheeling that uses fairly intelligent people who actually do a good job. I give them a little extra to make sure they'll come back, but other than that, I haven't had any problems getting that room or any of the others professionally cleaned."

It took her a while before she was able to ask her next question. "Did Margaret Freedman have a special name for that room?"

Bryan smiled. "As a matter of fact, yes. She called it her "Enlightenment Room.""

Chapter 10

What Bryan Grant had just said sounded fantastic.

Lynn couldn't help wondering if the beautiful lady who'd appeared to her in the bedroom had actually been the woman they were talking about.

"You seem more than slightly confused." Bryan grinned. "I can't say as I blame you."

"It's certainly a lot to think about," she said. "I'm not so sure I can comprehend something like an actual "Enlightenment Room."   It sounds so…fairytale-like."

"It does, doesn't it?"

Even so, she couldn't help fending off the many questions that had been building up inside her.

"You've been in this room?" she asked. "I mean, recently?"

"As I said, I've paid good money to have every room in the house professionally cleaned. As you've undoubtedly noticed, I haven't had the foyer or the high ceilings tended to yet, but I've recently located a Wheeling service that specializes in stuff like that, and a crew is due to show in a day or so."

"And you said there's nothing weird or special about that one room?"

"You sound surprised."

"I just thought…well, I guess I thought that with all the traffic Margaret had brought in there, there should be something about it that…" She felt a little embarrassed and didn't know how exactly to continue. "I guess I didn't know what I expected."

"I totally understand. And you're right. It is definitely a lot to think about."

***

After the dishes were washed and the leftovers put into the refrigerator, Bryan took Lynn out back to show her the ten-acre property, which led to a long gravel driveway sweeping down the hill in the back to the main road that went directly to Bridgeport.

A late-model charcoal-gray BMW sat in a two-car garage at the far end of the house. An aged gazebo embellished the back yard, where evidence of a flower garden dug up long ago encircled it.

Bryan was talking about the house and the property itself when he suddenly pulled his cell out of his jacket pocket. He read the display. He smiled sheepishly. "I'm sorry, but I've got to take this. I should only be a couple of minutes."

"It's okay. I'll be all right."

Bryan turned away. The phone pressed to his ear, he wandered off toward the heavily wooded section behind the garage.

She watched him as he walked away. Something quickly caught her eye, and she turned back to the house.

The beautiful redheaded lady dressed in white was standing just a few yards away, smiling brightly at her.

***

87

Lynn waited until Bryan had disappeared behind a grove of pine trees.

She turned to the lady. "You're Miss Margaret Freedman, aren't you?" She was surprised she was able to get the question out without difficulty.

"Yes, dear. I most certainly am."

A horde of butterflies appeared from out of nowhere, flitting directly toward the redheaded lady. Dozens swarmed closer, fluttering around her, some landing on her shoulders while others danced on her hair and tapped her cheekbones. A few even touched her lips and appeared to be kissing her.

"Where'd *they* come from?" Lynn asked, mesmerized. "I didn't see any sign of them until I started talking to you."

"One of the many perks of being a benevolent spirit," the woman said, smiling.

A benevolent spirit. Lynn didn't know if she should be shocked or frightened. This lady had just called herself a spirit. This meant she was dead.

But that can't possibly be, she thought wildly. *She's standing right there, and she's talking to me!*

A pink-winged dragonfly landed on the tip of the spirit lady's nose, staying there for only a moment before scurrying away.

"Dragonflies, too?" Lynn asked, confused.

Margaret Freedman nodded. "And birds, as well. Birds will often visit me when I'm out here, looking after the flowers I once tended to while I was living in your sphere. Cardinals, usually. But since I've passed over, my dragonflies and butterflies keep me company whenever I come back

88

for a visit. They especially love it when I walk down the hill to spend a quiet afternoon in the apple orchard just down the path." She tilted her head and smiled. Her long red hair slid down her shoulder. Half a dozen dragonflies hopped around on it the moment the sun reflected on it. "Do you like dragonflies, dear?"

"Oh, yes. They're beautiful and gentle, and they always seem to make me happy whenever I see them. I love them."

"Butterflies, too?"

"Especially butterflies."

The woman smiled, obviously pleased. "I figured you would."

"Really?"

"I've always been extremely perceptive, dear. Just one of the many rewards of practicing white magic."

As Lynn stared at her, she struggled to decide once again if the woman she was talking to was indeed there. Lynn had never seen a spirit before, let alone communicated with one. This was becoming more and more surreal. If it wasn't for the things Bryan had told her, she might have thought she'd died sometime during the night and had entered the spirit world.

But she was certain she was still alive. At least, she believed she was. To make sure, she tapped herself on the cheek.

"You're very much alive, my dear." The lady obviously understood Lynn's dilemma.

"Just checking," she said, a little embarrassed.

"I totally understand."

Lynn couldn't believe this spirit was a witch. It just didn't seem possible. Lynn knew very little about good witches and could only visualize them in the same context as Glinda, in the classic *The Wizard of Oz* movie. The other witches she'd been familiar with were those she'd seen in scary movies and read about in fairy tales as a child. She'd learned that they were nasty, cursed souls conjuring up evil spells and hexes that hurt and killed people they didn't like.

This lady could be nothing like them. For one thing, she was beautiful. And nice. And very comforting.

"You seem very confused, my dear."

Confused was a good word. In fact, it was the most appropriate word she could think of that could describe her feelings. She just couldn't imagine this lovely lady being anything but pleasant and hospitable. The kind of soul who would go out of her way to help anyone less fortunate, or desperately needing help.

Then she remembered the things Bryan had said. This lady had once cured people, helping them with their problems. People in love came to her and asked her to work her magic on them so they could stay together forever.

This kind of magic could never be a bad thing.

But she still found that she couldn't grasp any of this.

"What's confusing you, child?" Margaret Freedman asked.

"I imagine it's just my perception. You're not exactly what I would imagine a witch would be."

"You expect me to be ugly? With a gigantic wart on my chin? Dressed in black? Carrying a broomstick?"

Once again, Lynn felt foolish.

"Do you know *anything* about witches, child? Have you done any research on them?"

"I only know what I've seen in horror flicks or read in fairy tales."

"Most people think just as you do. Unfortunately, most are wrong. You see, there are many forms of witchcraft. And, consequently, many different varieties of witches."

"That makes sense."

"And since there are so many different varieties of witches, one must consider the fact that some are good. Not all witches are evil, my dear."

"That makes sense, too."

"This should also suggest to you that not all witches are necessarily good. *Or* bad. There is black magic, of course—which everyone knows is very bad. But there is also white magic—which is very, very good."

"I can tell you're definitely not bad at all."

"What makes you say that, dear?"

"Your eyes. Your smile. Your softness. The fact that I feel very comfortable, relaxed and warm here, with you. There is nothing cold or dark about you." Lynn hoped she'd expressed herself accurately. "Am I right?"

"Yes, my dear. You are. And I was right, as well."

"What do you mean?"

"When I first saw you out front, hiding from those two drunken idiots, I could tell you were one very special young woman."

"You could?"

"Your name is Lynn, isn't it, dear?"

"How did you know—"

The woman just smiled.

"You must have been eavesdropping when Bryan and I were talking in the kitchen."

Still smiling, Margaret Freedman said, "When you've passed, my dear, eavesdropping comes quite naturally. It also very often comes in handy."

"Is there anything else you know about me?" Lynn asked.

"A great many things. First of all, you have recently suffered a terrible blow."

"H-How did you…how'd you know *that*?"

"As I just said, I can see things. Correct me if I'm wrong. You have recently learned that your boyfriend was unfaithful. Is this true?"

It took her some time to respond. She stared at the woman, not knowing how to express what was in her heart. But somehow, telling this lady about her recent experience—or anything else, for that matter—didn't seem so difficult. Margaret Freedman made her feel very comfortable. Lynn suspected she could tell the spirit lady anything. "Yes. He was."

"With someone very close to you, I assume…"

Feeling a sudden surge of anger, Lynn nodded.

"I understand, child."

"You do?"

"I also understand why you've come here."

"Actually, I was brought here by those two...those Pozner boys. Against my will. And as soon as I was able to get away from them, I came here and hid in that grove out front—"

"I'd already figured that out when I saw you climbing the hill. What I meant was, I know why you came here instead of running down the other side of the hill."

"I felt kind of funny, snooping around on someone else's property. Besides, I didn't know what was behind the house. I stopped close to the top of the hill, where the bushes were thick enough to conceal me. By this time, I was pretty tired. I guess I decided that grove was a really great place to hide and rest for a while..."

"Are you sure this is why you stayed hidden so close to the house? And why you chose to come in—even though no one answered the door?"

Lynn struggled to remember what had gone through her mind during her flight. For some reason, she just couldn't recall why she'd chosen the house as a sanctuary rather than explore the backyard.

"I honestly don't remember," she said.

"You actually came here to see me." Several butterflies appeared, fluttering excitedly around the woman's flaming red mane.

Lynn didn't respond. She could only stare at the sudden activity.

"I had a feeling someone would be coming to visit me. I also had a feeling that this someone would be a lovely young woman. And that we'd get along very well."

"But how could you possibly know about me, or that I would—"

"I just did, my dear. I had a feeling many years ago that this would happen."

"You had…a premonition? Years ago?"

"I sensed that one day many years down the road, a lovely young woman would come to my house. I also sensed that this same woman would be able to see me and talk to me, even though I'd passed into the next sphere."

Lynn studied the woman's face and wondered how she could have possibly predicted such a strange event from so long ago. What she saw in the lady's beautiful blue eyes told her that she truly believed what she'd just said.

But it didn't make any sense. Lynn had no idea she'd be coming here. If she hadn't been kidnapped, this situation wouldn't have even happened, and she wouldn't have ended up anywhere near this place.

"But how could you know so many years ago that—"

"Sorry about that." Bryan appeared around the corner, pocketing his cell as he approached her. "Just some bit of business with my Pittsburgh office. I didn't mean to leave you here alone."

"I wasn't—" She caught herself and stopped. And bit her lower lip.

"Pardon me?"

"I was just going to say that it wasn't a problem. It's actually very quiet and peaceful out here."

"It is, isn't it?" He gave the yard a quick scan. "It's a real shame I can't convince anyone else how beautiful and serene it is here." He paused for a moment. "You wouldn't, by any chance, know anyone who might be interested in buying this place, would you?"

She didn't know anyone who would enjoy living in such a remote area, especially with people like the Pozners for neighbors. "Sorry. The people I know and deal with are already settled."

He sighed. "Just talking out loud. Frustration does that, sometimes."

She nodded.

"Let's go back inside. I could use more fresh coffee. How about you?"

"Actually, I'd love to have a shower, if that's all right." She looked down at herself and frowned. "These clothes…"

"Yeah, crawling around in the dirt and hiding in the bushes tends to put a little wear'n tear on the old duds. How about if I make a fresh pot while you do what you need to do? I'll make sure you've got enough towels and whatever else you might need."

"This is very nice of you."

"It's no trouble."

Chapter 11

The spirit of Margaret Freedman appeared once again, as Lynn followed Bryan into the kitchen.

The beautiful redhead hovered in front of the window, watching them as they went back out into the dining room. She said nothing, just kept smiling as Lynn crossed the room and went back out into the foyer.

"I'll get you fresh towels from the linen closet," Bryan said as he led the way up the stairs.

"The towels I used earlier will be just fine," she said.

"They weren't exactly fresh. A little musty, actually. I found a working washer and dryer in the laundry room down in the basement. I've been using them, but they're both very old and obviously hadn't been used in years. I asked one of the cleaning people to hose them down, then add in some old towels and washrags and a little soap to clean them out and get them working again. They still function, but the cycles take forever handling anything but small loads. I honestly didn't count on having company. I could do your clothes if you like, but you wouldn't have anything to wear but my housecoat in the meantime. And it could take at least an hour before they're dry enough to put back on."

"It's all right. I can stand wearing these until I get back to my place. I appreciate the offer, though."

Bryan disappeared in a room at the end of the hall and came back a few moments later carrying two large white bath towels, a white washcloth and a bar of soap. He handed them over. "Just in case the towels you used before haven't dried yet. I'll be down in the kitchen. I've got a couple of business calls to make, so…" He smiled. "Take all the time you need."

"Thank you *so* much."

"No problem." He turned and went back down the stairs.

***

After placing the fresh towels on the edge of the sink, Lynn pulled back the moldy shower curtain.

The tub was very old—one of those claw-footed things they used to make years ago. Its center had yellowed with age and rust but would be all right for a quick shower. She turned on the hot tap. The water dribbled out in a weak stream, but she expected that from a place that hadn't been fully functional. She turned the middle tap. The shower spray came out just as shakily, sputtering at first, then finally providing a light cascade. After adjusting the temperature by flicking on the cold, she took off her dirty clothes and draped them over the edge of the sink. Then, picking up the washcloth and soap Bryan had provided, she stepped into the tub and pulled the curtain shut.

Ten minutes later, she toweled dry and put her clothes back on. She debated about what she should do with her hair. After blotting it gently with a towel, she carefully pushed her fingers through it and decided to let it dry on its own. It didn't look too bad. And anyway, who would care? Bryan was interested only in sending her on her way so he could get back to selling the house. Even so, after what she'd endured the day before, she knew it would be quite a while before she went back to caring about how she looked. It would also be some time before she decided to start dating again, let alone pursuing another serious relationship.

She stepped away from the smudged mirror and opened the door.

The spirit of Margaret Freedman appeared out in the hall, smiling at her.

***

Lynn discovered that she wasn't frightened at all. Perhaps it was because she'd experienced only warmth and a strong sense of contentment whenever Margaret Freedman appeared to her. Whatever it was, she discovered that she was very curious about this beautiful spirit and wanted to find out more about her.

"Why are you visiting me again?" Not wanting Bryan to hear her, she spoke very softly.

"I had a feeling you'd want to see me again," the spirit lady said. "That's why I appeared to you in the kitchen a little while ago."

"Why didn't you say anything?"

"In front of *him*?" Margaret Freedman laughed. "He would have thought you were touched, dear child."

"I take it he isn't able to see you at all?"

"He did tell you he wasn't superstitious? Didn't he? That he didn't believe in a lot of stuff that he obviously considers nonsense?"

"Yes…"

"Non-believers cannot see me or even sense my presence. I don't believe that boy felt anything even when I passed through him more than a dozen times during the last few days to see what was going on in his head."

"He seems very nice, though."

"He is. He is extremely nice and well-mannered. His parents brought him up properly. We are all very proud of Bryan."

"We?"

"The family, child. The Grants have always been a very honorable, respected group. Bryan's father was a reputable real estate broker based in Wheeling for more than thirty years before he passed. Bryan's mother was also very well-thought-of. I believe she was high up on the Board of Education in the Wheeling schools. She taught high school English and History for many years."

"Were they non-believers, too?"

"Bryan's father, as I recall, didn't believe at all in any of the supernatural forces. Bryan's mother, Diana, however, was a great believer in white magic. This was most likely because her mother, who knew me very well, actually approved of the practice."

"Bryan told me many things about you."

Margaret Freedman smiled. "I was there when he was telling you all he'd learned from others. And

99

from whatever research he did. I'm not exactly sure why he found it necessary to do all that research—especially since just a couple of phone calls to his aunts would have given him whatever answers he needed, mind you. I can only assume that he did it just to use whatever he'd gleaned as a selling point in his campaign to rid himself of my house."

"I take it you don't want him to sell?"

A slender vertical line appeared between her reddish brows. "This house has been in the family for more than a century, dear. I have always loved living here, and I'm quite sure it has always loved my living here, as well. The two of us have shared many, many years of treasured, unforgettable memories. Besides, it happens to be our family's heritage. Its legacy. Have you noticed the furniture?"

"Yes. The hutches and cabinets in the dining room are very beautiful."

"Much of that stuff was shipped over here from England many years ago. Bryan wouldn't think twice of selling every single scrap of it to the many local flea markets in Wheeling and Bridgeport. I love the boy dearly, but unfortunately, he has succumbed to the phoniness of his generation."

"I don't think he feels any sort of connection," Lynn said. "I guess it's because he's lived in Pittsburgh for such a long time. His business is there. He obviously has no ties to this area at all."

"You are correct, my dear. I have tried using my powers to influence his decisions, but since he is a non-believer…" She just shrugged.

"Was Bryan correct about what he said?"

"What specifically are you talking about, dear?"

Lynn hesitated.

"You can ask me anything, child. This is why I've come to you."

"Why *did* you come to me? You said it was because you sensed that I wanted to talk to you. Is this true? Or is there some other reason?"

The woman went silent, watching Lynn intently. "As I've told you before, I've felt a closeness to you ever since you climbed the hill. And the more we talk, the more I've been acquiring an even stronger feeling."

"What sort of feeling?"

"I've been experiencing a true sense of a kindred spirit connection with you."

"Is that possible? I mean, did you start feeling it when I first came here?"

"Before that, child."

"Before I climbed the hill?"

The spirit lady smiled. "Long before, dear."

Lynn couldn't help wondering how the woman could have possibly experienced such a strange connection—especially long before meeting her. "Really? How? How could you—"

"The important thing, child, is that the two of us have connected. A connection such as this doesn't happen very often. When it does, it should be treasured, nurtured, taken advantage of. And now that we seem to have this special link between us, I feel comfortable telling you that whatever you ask me, I shall not hesitate to answer. And, I might add, I will never lie to you."

Although Lynn truly believed what this woman had just told her, she was still hesitant to ask her about what Bryan had told her.

"What is it you wish to ask, my dear? I can see in your eyes that whatever it is, is very important to you."

Lynn wanted to ask the spirit lady about the Enlightenment Room. However, she didn't quite know how to go about it. But even though she was hesitant, she found that her curiosity would eventually win out.

After a few moments, Margaret Freedman smiled. "Does this have anything to do with my Enlightenment Room?"

Lynn felt her cheeks redden. She couldn't help thinking that the spirit lady could read her thoughts. It was unnerving, to say the least. And it made her feel even more vulnerable.

"Are you afraid to ask me, child?"

Lynn found that she still couldn't speak.

Margaret Freedman continued watching her. Lynn suspected that the spirit lady was making another quick but thorough evaluation. Then, smiling, the woman said, "Would you like me to tell you about?"

Before Lynn could respond, the spirit lady said, "Or would you like me to *show* it to you?"

Chapter 12

The room awaited them just a few feet down the hall.

Its door was unlocked. Even so, Lynn felt uneasy about opening it.

Margaret moved closer. In a soft, caressing whisper, she said, "Go ahead and open it, child. You can't very well see the room without first opening the door."

"I guess I'm just nervous." Lynn realized how foolish she was acting. But she had to admit that it was intimidating, entering a room where so many people had gone inside so many years ago to experience things that would ultimately change their lives forever.

Margaret smiled. "There's nothing in that room you should be afraid of, child. In fact, there's nothing in there that would be of any interest to anyone nowadays, I'm afraid." Margaret was still smiling, but Lynn could sense a deep sadness emanating from the lady's spirit. "My potions, essential oils, enhancing scents, spells, vitamins, medicines..." She shook her head. "All my artwork—the landscapes, the mountain scenes I did many years ago and loved so much... Everything was removed ages ago. Much of it was sold, while everything else was either destroyed or distributed among the family as keepsakes. This special place is now no different from any other room in this house."

"But Bryan said he sensed something dark in here…"

"I heard what the boy said, child."

"But if he is a non-believer, how could he possibly—"

"The forces of the spirit world can be extremely powerful." The spirit lady's smile vanished instantly. "Even non-believers can sense something in the presence of this darkness."

"But he said it was the stale air, probably because the windows hadn't been opened in such a long—"

"Non-believers often create silly excuses for things they cannot understand." The smile quickly returned to Margaret's face. "They are quite ingenious in that respect."

"What about all the rumors Bryan told me about this room?" Lynn asked.

"You will understand a great many things the moment you open the door," Margaret said, her smile deepening.

"Are you sure it's okay? I mean, with Bryan?"

"Believe me, my dear, he will be preoccupied with his business concerns for quite a while."

"You're sure?"

"I've seen that boy spend hours at a time on that little phone of his. Yes, child. I'm quite certain you're no longer his main concern."

Lynn still felt some uneasiness. "So then, when I open the door and go inside, I'll just be in a room no different from the others?"

"Not necessarily."

"Whatever do you mean?"

"My child, if I have been correct in my evaluation of you, you'll experience things most others would never be able to comprehend in a lifetime."

Lynn sensed the fear scurrying back. "Are you saying there really is something different about this room? Even after all these years? Even though everything special was taken out of it?"

"Let's just go on in and see what happens, okay?"

Lynn didn't move.

Margaret laughed. "Child, I promise you nothing in that room will harm you."

Taking a breath, Lynn reached for the glass doorknob. Touching it made her tremble, but she kept her wits about her, remembering that the same thing had happened on the front porch when she'd first touched the front door.

"I'm being silly again," she said, her frustration growing again.

"Open the door, child. It will not bite you."

Suddenly angry at herself, Lynn grasped the knob and turned it. Her pulse began fluttering the moment she gently eased open the door.

***

At first glance, the room looked pretty much like the one Laura had slept in.

A large double bed extended from the opposite wall. An ancient dresser and vanity covered most of the wall on her right, a large built-in closet on her left. Sunlight flickered in through the sheer white drapes over the large bay window. Other than its stuffiness, which Bryan had already mentioned, there was nothing different or strange about this room.

However, the moment Lynn crossed the threshold, she realized that it indeed *felt* very different. A strong sensation of warmth fell over her like a comforting blanket, making her tingly all over. The stuffiness quickly vanished, replaced by heavenly aromas and scents. Instead of turning around and running back out into the hall, she found that she could not move. It wasn't that she was unable to; she discovered that she didn't *want* to. This strange sensation was just as irresistible as it was overwhelming, its warmth and the delicious mix of sweet scents intoxicating. She stood very still, her eyes closed, the warmth cascading over her as if a smooth, caressing mist of sunshine had dropped dazzling pieces of radiance gently onto her.

As she bathed herself in this delicious vision, other bizarre sensations drifted by, filling her mind with ambiances. The deliciousness of a sensuous kiss. The ecstatic pleasure of passionate lovemaking. Loud, unbridled laughter. Bright, ecstatic smiles. Sparkling eyes. Dazzling rays of sunshine. The majestic beauty of a gleaming rainbow. The calming sound of a distant waterfall. Intense warmth. Total release. A feeling of ultimate euphoria.

She sensed no hint of darkness amongst the images. Felt no suggestion of cold. No feelings of anger, of betrayal. No hatred. Or envy. Or frustration.

She wanted to stay here forever, wrapped up tightly in this cocoon of blissful ecstasy...

The moment that thought entered her mind, she heard Margaret Freedman's voice.

"Bathe yourself in this miraculous rapture, child. Let it envelop you, fill you with happiness... But never let it leave you...never let go of it...or lose it...or ignore it—not even for a single moment..."

"How can this be?" she thought, confused, and frightened. *"How can this be happening?"*

"For one very simple reason, my child. I have just given it to you."

"But what have I done to deserve this?'

"You have come to me at a very crucial time. You have come to me at a time when all this wonder, this magnificence, must be preserved forever."

"Is it because Bryan is selling the house?"

"It is much more than that, child. It is because we have become kindred spirits. Since I have long passed, I wish to pass on some of my gifts to someone who is deserving. And now that our paths have crossed, I find that I would like you to experience what I once possessed."

Lynn found that her fear and confusion had returned. *"And just what is that? I can't possibly carry on what you were doing, can I? Your gifts...well, they belonged to you. Didn't they?"*

107

"Yes, child. They were my very own special gifts. And no, you cannot possibly duplicate what I spent my entire mortal life practicing."

"Then what can I—"

"Since I now exist only in spiritual form, I am no longer be able to preserve any of the wonders that remain in this room. But once I pass them on to you, they will live within you."

Lynn still could not comprehend what the spirit lady was telling her. But she somehow sensed that Margaret Freedman was referring to something very important, and that it was essential to find out exactly what it was.

"But how can I possibly...I have no idea how to deal with any of this."

"The benevolent forces will guide you, my dear. Do not worry."

"What will happen? Will I be changed?"

"Your spiritual essence has been elevated, and you will no longer feel the same."

"That frightens me. I mean, it should, shouldn't it?"

"Do not be frightened. What is happening to you is a very wonderful but rare phenomenon. While you are in possession of its gift, you will not need anything else."

"But what is all this? What will happen to me?"

"It is total and complete euphoria. It is the nirvana of the spirit that only a very select few have experienced."

"But why me? What makes me so deserving of all this?"

"I've already told you that we are connected, my dear. I sensed this connection the moment I saw you, and I am never wrong. And the more I talked with you, the more I was convinced that I did indeed find my true kindred spirit."

"But what will I...am I going to be a witch like you?"

"No, child. You are only to use what you have been given as you see fit."

"What have I been given? I don't understand. I feel warmth and comfort, but—"

"Do you feel anger?"

"No..."

"Darkness? Cold? Hatred? Resentment? Terror? Fear? Pain? Any of the dark elements that have been set loose into the Universe by the Black Powers?"

"Actually, I feel better than I can ever remember."

"This is good, my dear. It means you are accepting the brightest and most dazzling effects of my wonderful gift. You see, this room is filled with its own very special magic. Everyone who has come here was in search of their own ultimate happiness. Many were truly in love, while others had lost their love and needed guidance to help them cope with their loss. Still others had lost their way and came here to find it again."

"That's what all this is? Love?"

"Among other things, yes. The brightest and warmest of all auras continues to exist in this room. And it has been this way for many years. It will

always be this way—that is, for true believers. Since I've granted everyone's wishes, the strength of their love—as well as their own individual aura—grew much stronger. And when they left, a small portion of their love essence remained here, in this room. "

"What about all the bad stuff? Didn't anyone ever come in here with bad Karma? With misfortune? With loss?"

"Yes, child. And like the others, I'm sorry to say that portions of their darkness remain here to this day."

"I sensed sadness and torment when I first came in. And I might have heard crying. But it was very distant—almost as if it wasn't really there, or about to fade away. And after just a few moments, I no longer experienced any of it."

"The sadness and torment clung to many of the auras that entered this room. Using my potions and spells, I exorcised those desperately needing it. Since these negatives had nowhere else to go, it was only natural that they remain in this room. I'd always hoped they would have dissolved long before now. But as I said before, the dark forces are extremely powerful. They are still here—quite possibly because this room has remained closed for so long, and the windows have been sealed shut. But at least they're not nearly as potent as they once were. Apparently, time has been a friend to us in this respect."

"Like I said, the dark feelings were very distant."

"My presence has helped considerably, child. The darkness has always dimmed in the brightness of my warmth."

"I guess they'd be stronger if I was in this room alone, then?"

"The important thing is that you don't feel or sense any of that now. You don't, do you?"

Lynn suddenly went silent, using her senses to pick up anything dark or unpleasant. She soon found that she could only experience the brightness and the warmth. Her feeling of euphoria remained strong. *"I really don't."*

"This is very good. It also helps that you are a pure spirit. And why I have chosen you to enter this very special room."

"This darkness... Is this what Bryan felt when he came in here?"

"Non-believers always seem to sense the darkness, the anger, the hate, and the hopelessness. Their negative auras easily accept the darkness, which shuts out the warmth, the light, the tenderness—all the miracles needed so desperately to achieve true happiness."

"Do I have to worry about this darkness? I mean, when I leave, will it—"

"All darkness will continue to remain here, in this room, as long as you wish it to."

"Then the darkness will never stay with me?"

"Only if you let it inside you."

"Why would I?"

"Most mortals carry around their weaknesses much more easily than their strengths. And if you let

111

in their own personal darkness, it will eventually push away all the warmth and brightness you are carrying inside you."

"That sounds terrible."

"It is human nature, child. But I wouldn't worry, if I were you. Since you have entered my special room as my kindred spirit, the bright, wonderfully warm auras have claimed you. Let them cling tightly to you. Never let them go. And they will continue to become one with your essence."

"You mean—"

"As long as you accept this special gift, child, nothing bad will ever happen to you again..."

***

Lynn opened her eyes and found that she was standing out in the hall, facing the closed door of the Enlightenment Room.

She rubbed her eyes and tried focusing. She remembered opening the door and walking in. That happened just a few minutes ago.

Well, didn't it?

She also remembered that the room looked no different from the one she'd woken up in. There were no signs of supernatural goings-on, no bookcase filled with bottles of special lotions. No books on witchcraft. Or spells. Just a bed, a dresser, some furniture...

Then she realized she was alone.

Alarmed, she turned around and scanned the hall.

Nothing. No one. She was all by herself.

Where had the spirit lady gone?

"M-Margaret?" Frightened and confused, she scanned the hall once again. "A-Are you here anywhere?"

The heavy silence responded loudly, unnerving her.

"Please, Margaret, please tell me... Where'd you go?"

More dead silence.

Alarmed, she tried to remember what had happened in that room. The only thing that registered was that she'd felt slightly different the instant she'd entered.

Warmer. More comfortable. Content.

And for some strange, inexplicable reason, she still felt much happier than she could ever remember.

What happened in there?

It must have been really extreme to make her feel so different.

So why couldn't she remember?

She tried recalling the experience once again. This time, she struggled to visualize walking in there. Looking for things that would explain the situation better. An item that might clear up a few important matters.

And once again coming up empty.

The room had a big double bed. And a vanity. And an antique dresser. And a bay window, where the afternoon sun came in through the sheer white drapes. Nothing out of the ordinary at all.

But even so, something was off.

Margaret had urged her to enter the room. The spirit lady had followed her in and spoken to her. She'd told her about the room. And what had gone on. And why it was so different from all the other rooms in the house. Then—

What had she done after that?

She just couldn't remember what happened. Or where Margaret had gone.

Had the spirit lady disappeared? Moved into a different sphere the moment Lynn had gone back out into the hall?

Why can't I remember leaving the room? Or even closing the door?

Had something in the room caused this horrible blackout in her brain?

Why couldn't she remember anything?

Struggling even harder to make her mind work, she visualized the spirit lady's voice entering her thoughts, telling her to—

To what?

What had the spirit lady said?

She closed her eyes and tried very hard to overcome the frightening blankness that had mysteriously taken over. There shouldn't be a problem figuring this out, should there? She'd never had a problem remembering anything before. She'd always been fortunate to have a wonderful memory. Besides, this all happened just minutes ago. There should be no logical reason why she couldn't recall every single detail that had transpired the moment she'd opened the door and walked into that room.

However, the only thing that registered was that Margaret Freedman had spoken to her.

So why can't I recall anything the spirit lady said?

Lynn rubbed the back of her neck. She'd been through a lot during the last twelve hours. It was no wonder her memory wasn't working correctly. She needed to gather whatever she could from any image registering in her brain.

But no matter how hard she tried, the pictures remained hazy and fleeting, at best.

What in heaven's name happened to my memory?

On impulse, she turned the knob, pushed open the door and stood in the doorway, staring at the empty room.

"Margaret?"

Nothing.

"Are you...are you still there?"

Silence.

Sighing, she pulled the door shut.

Exhaustion once again showed its ugly head. The last several hours had taken their toll. She needed relaxation—not unnecessary stress. The most sensible thing she could do was ask Bryan to drive her back to Wheeling so she could pick up her car. Then, after she returned to her apartment and enjoyed a large glass of wine and several hours of complete rest, she should just chill out. Once well rested, she could try to decide what had actually happened in the Enlightenment Room.

Right now, she saw no reason to agonize over anything. That would be handled later, after she'd had time to clear her mind of the last twelve hours.

Her mind set, she shuffled down the hall and began descending the stairs.

Bryan came out of the dining room. He had his cell in his hand. Seeing her, he stopped cold. "I was just about to come up and see if you were okay."

"I'm...just fine." She realized right then that she indeed felt fine. In fact, she discovered that she felt *more* than fine. She had no idea why, just that she felt wonderful and content. Her former state of exhaustion had apparently disappeared. And, for some curious reason, she actually felt completely revitalized.

The moment she reached the last few steps, she stopped. Bryan was staring at her. "Something wrong?"

His expression seemed cloudy. "I guess it was the shower."

The shower?

What on earth was he talking about?

"What about it?"

"You obviously needed one."

"Why would you say that?"

He smiled sheepishly. "You seem totally revitalized. In fact, you look a hundred percent better than you did when you left the kitchen."

"Thank you..." She had no idea how else to respond and decided to let it slide. She needed to get a move on.

"By the way, the coffee's ready. I also heated up some croissants, if you're hungry."

She instant felt guilty. Right now, food was the farthest thing from her mind. But this man had been good to her. She didn't want to hurt his feelings. "Thanks, but I'm still full from that sensational breakfast you fixed for us."

"You have room for coffee, don'tcha?"

"I can always find time to enjoy a cup of good coffee."

"Good deal. I was just about to pour myself a cup."

Chapter 13

Bryan poured coffee.

He set the coffeepot down on the counter and sat facing her at the table. He was sugaring his coffee when he began staring at her again.

"Now what's wrong?" she asked uneasily.

He didn't speak right off. He sat quite still, his spoon motionless in his left hand. Finally he said, "You sure do look…well, different. *Really* different…"

She immediately felt another tinge of embarrassment. "I thought we already went over this. My shower…"

"It's more than that. *Much* more."

"Just what are you getting at?"

"I honestly don't know."

Her thoughts went right back to the Enlightenment Room. She struggled once again to recall what happened. How could the simple act of entering a musty old room cause her appearance to change?

In spite of her efforts, all that came back was a feeling of warmth and contentment. That, plus the fact that when she'd left the room, she'd felt better than she had in a very long time.

But how would her strange experience alter someone else's perception of her? How would it change her outward appearance?

Frustrated, she had no idea how to handle this. "It was just a shower, you know."

"Even so, you look very, very different."

"But how?"

He returned the spoon to the sugar bowl and sat staring at her. Then, after considerable thought, he said, "You look like…like something very strange just happened to you."

That wasn't exactly what she wanted to hear. "Are you saying I look weird?"

"Nothing like that. Not at all."

"Then please explain what you mean."

He sat back. "If I hadn't seen you before you went upstairs just half an hour ago, I'd say that you look like a totally different person."

"Different how?"

His eyes stayed on her. She could tell he was having difficulty. "I know we've only known one another just a few hours… But honestly, I've never seen anyone look so…*happy*…"

He'd said it as if it was something he'd never said before.

Happy? Did he really mean it?

Or had something else happened that neither of them could explain?

"Really?"

"There's a brightness coming from you I never noticed before."

A brightness?

She could never remember a single time in her life when someone mentioned "a brightness" when referring to her. People usually thought she looked depressed, or despondent. Or, mostly, pensive.

She recalled that one embarrassingly awkward summer, when she'd shot up more than three inches in height but didn't add a single ounce to her frame. Then the next year, when her face had transformed into a network of disgusting, unsightly zits. The blemishes finally went away during her senior year, but even after painstakingly tending to her hair, finding the best outfits for her slender figure and learning how to use makeup to look as presentable as possible, she could never forget the humiliating memory of being one of the last girls picked to attend her senior prom.

Due to emotional maturity and a sense of self-confidence she'd developed after earning her degree in Business Management, the last few years had done much to improve her overall appearance. But even though she'd managed to turn a few male heads, having a beautiful, extremely popular younger sister had done more harm in just a few short years than all the insults and humiliation she'd endured in high school. And the final incident with Ariana and Frank sealed the deal.

So how could she possibly explain what had happened in this house during the last half-hour?

How could Bryan Grant, a man she'd met just a few hours earlier, notice such brightness emanating from her?

And, even more importantly, why did she just discover that she no longer hated Ariana or Frank?

It was true. Although the hurt she'd experienced from their betrayal still tugged heavily at her heart, she no longer felt the anger or the rage that had beset her since the incident. She had no idea why; she knew only that she no longer experienced the same dark, seething heat that had consumed her the day before. The hurt remained but did not sting quite so severely.

She felt happy. And, more importantly, she just learned that she even *looked* happy. With a brightness coming from her that could be seen by a stranger. And those dark, heated emotions were gone. Totally.

"You seem confused." Bryan was staring again.

"I guess I am."

"Why?"

She shrugged. "No one has ever said I looked *happy* before."

"Never?"

She shook her head.

"I find that strange."

She found that this conversation was growing more and more bizarre. "Why is that?"

He reddened. "I don't know. I guess I said the wrong thing, didn't I?"

"Please. Just answer my question."

He shrugged. "Maybe it's because I've never seen you in this light before." He picked up his coffee cup and took a long, reflective sip. "I really feel stupid, too."

"About what?"

"Well, for one thing, not noticing how beautiful your eyes are. Generally, I notice a person's eyes first. I've been doing that since I was a kid. I mean, it's a perfectly natural thing to do—especially when you're talking directly to them. And in the insurance business, you meet and talk to a *lot* of people. But as I said—" He shrugged a shoulder.

"You think my eyes…are beautiful?"

"Very."

She wondered if he was telling the truth. It took her only a moment to realize he was. There was something in his own eyes—or body language—that told her he was sincere. Whatever it was, she could definitely tell that this man honestly thought she had beautiful eyes.

But why did she look and feel so happy?

Her curiosity quickly became overwhelming, and she realized right at that moment that there was one sure way to solve this puzzle. She got up. "I have to use the bathroom. I'll be right back."

***

The moment Lynn stepped into the bathroom just off the kitchen, closed the door and faced the mirror, she realized something had indeed changed.

Something mysterious had definitely happened to her in the Enlightenment Room. And the moment she drew closer to the mirror, she discovered what it was.

It was her face. No longer just pretty or, at best, reasonably attractive, it now glowed with a radiance she'd never seen before.

And when she focused on her eyes, she discovered the same sort of shimmering metamorphosis.

No longer a lackluster shade of light green, they now gleamed a beautifully rich emerald green, sparkling the instant the bathroom light touched on them.

Shocked and a little frightened, she stepped back. Then, gathering courage, she moved closer, until her waist touched the edge of the sink. And then she noticed something else that made no sense.

It was her hair, which had always been a mousey brown. Even after weekly sessions at the salon, she had never been able to get it looking good enough to be worthy of anyone's attention. But now she discovered that it had become a rich chestnut glistening majestically in the bathroom lighting.

What's happened to me?

Why, at thirty-two, do I suddenly look like...a babe?

Had something truly magical happened to her in the Enlightenment Room?

Had something changed her so drastically that it had altered her appearance?

It had to have been something like that. It couldn't have been anything else.

But what was it? Some sort of miracle?

Her pulse fluttering, she closed her eyes and tried once again to recall every single detail.

The room had once been a special place, yet it hadn't been locked. Margaret had told her that it was now no different from any of the other rooms.

"There's nothing in that room you should be afraid of..."

According to Margaret, there was nothing in there that would be of interest to anyone.

123

Then, after much hesitation and fear, Lynn had opened the door and gone in. And realized instantly that the spirit lady had been telling her the truth. As she'd said, the room was no different from any of the others. It had a bed. And a dresser. And a closet. And a large bay window.

The room was very similar to the one Lynn had slept in.

But something just didn't make sense. Even though the room looked no different than the others, there *had* to be something special about it... Something that couldn't be seen. Or sensed. Or even noticed.

Because whatever there was that made it different had somehow changed Lynn's inner being, as well as her appearance.

It was called the Enlightenment Room. That fact alone meant it was different. That it was special.

She opened her eyes and found that she was gazing into the dazzling, emerald green eyes of the striking-looking woman in the mirror.

That's me. I know it is because I'm right here, and I'm looking at my reflection... But it doesn't seem like my reflection because I don't ever remember looking this good.

Or feeling this good...

Something magical had taken place in that room.

It had to have been, because whatever it was had done something very strange to her memory.

Maybe whatever had happened was all emotional. The miracles might have taken place from within. Emotions. Feelings. Sensations. Recollections. Perceptions.

She closed her eyes once again, trying even harder to focus.

Had she felt warmth? Contentment? Euphoria? Satisfaction? Happiness?

Yes. All of those things.

Enlightenment. The truest sense of Nirvana. For some reason she couldn't begin to fathom, something had happened that cleansed her of all negative emotions, changing her on the inside, which also altered her outward appearance.

Margaret Freedman had been in that room with her. The spirit lady had followed her inside...

She'd said things to me. Wonderful things. Things that made me feel special...and happy...and content...

Lynn struggled to recall exactly what the spirit lady had said. Again, nothing came to her that could explain these changes.

The only other thing she could remember was the fact that she wasn't in there very long. Just a few minutes, as an educated guess. If it had been longer, Bryan might have thought something was wrong and rushed upstairs to make sure she was all right.

But it wasn't long at all. Just a few minutes ago, in the kitchen, Bryan had mentioned half an hour from the time she'd left him to have her shower. This told her that, allowing ten minutes or

125

so for her shower, she wasn't in the Enlightenment Room much longer than fifteen minutes.

She'd gone in there with Margaret and, what felt like just moments later, discovered that she was standing out in the hall. By herself.

With no sign of Margaret Freedman anywhere.

This left her with the same haunting question as before.

Where had the spirit lady gone?

***

Bryan sat at the kitchen table, watching her curiously as she came back into the room. He jabbed a thumb at the coffeepot. "Refill?"

"Thanks, but I don't think so. I really need to get back to Wheeling as soon as possible. I have to see if my car's where I parked it. Or sitting on blocks."

He smiled. "Hopefully, it'll be all right." He had one last sip of coffee. "Sure. Whatever you wanna do. Are you sure you don't want a croissant?"

"I'm good, thanks. And I really appreciate all you've done."

"I was glad to help. How soon did you want to leave?"

"As soon as possible, if you don't mind."

He glanced at the ancient wall clock above the stove. "Wheeling's just about twenty minutes from here. With light traffic, it's really not much of a problem. But since it's approaching the dinner hour..." He shrugged.

"I know. I'm sorry about that."

126

"No worries. Even at this time of day, Wheeling traffic is nowhere near as bad as that mess in downtown Pittsburgh. I'm sure we'll be able to make it back to your car by seven. Since it's Saturday, rush shouldn't be bad at all. On the other hand, we need to get there before the party crowd staggers in to make things crazy." He got up and put his cup and saucer on the counter. "We can be ready to go in a couple of minutes, if that's okay…"

"Sounds good to me."

Chapter 14

Lynn's copper Honda Accord sat along the curb in front of the furniture store, where she'd left it more than twenty-four hours earlier. A tow truck was parked directly behind it, the long bed of the rig pulled up close to the rear of the car.

Its lights blinking, a police car sat parked alongside the Honda, causing traffic to veer carefully around it. The lanky cop standing behind the squad car busily scribbled a ticket from his thick pad while the tow truck operator removed his equipment from his truck and prepared to secure the rear axle to enable the Honda to be pulled onto his rig.

"Just in time." Bryan frowned as he parked the BMW beside the curb two spaces down. "I guess now you can personally thank them for moving it for you."

"At least it's still in one piece." Lynn found that she wasn't as angry or as frustrated as she should have been. She considered herself fortunate that vandals hadn't trashed the car or stripped it of its tires and left it on blocks. And as she got out of the BMW, she strongly sensed that this situation might turn out all right.

"Nothing bad will ever happen to you again..."

She closed the door and paused the instant that fleeting thought entered her mind.

What was that? she wondered as the warm feeling swept through her. *A premonition? Or just a glimmer of hope?*

"Want some backup?" Bryan pushed open his door as she crossed in front of the BMW. "They might take you more seriously if I was right there with you." He shrugged. "You know how guys are, right?"

"Thanks." She smiled. "I've got this."

"You sure? I promise I'll be very polite and non-threatening. I can even toss out a few impressive legal terms that might rattle them a little."

"I think I'll be all right."

He shook his head. "You sure don't look like someone about to have their car towed."

She smiled. "I just have this feeling that things will turn out."

The tow truck guy was young, maybe thirty, broad and thick, his gray overalls snug around his middle. His thick black beard was unkempt and dirty. His long black hair stuck out of his gray baseball cap and hung down just above his shoulders. Grease smudges stained his right cheek and forehead. His big hands were hidden by a thick pair of filthy tan gloves. The front of his cap said, *ED'S BODY SHOP*. He didn't acknowledge her presence as she drew closer.

"Are you Ed?" she asked.

She somehow sensed that this man had trouble with authority. She didn't know how she knew;

she'd picked up an unpleasant darkness emanating from him while watching him work.

"Not hardly," he muttered, getting his equipment ready.

"What's your name, then?"

"What's it to ya?"

His darkness had grown thicker, colder. Intense frustration flowed freely from him.

"Would it ruin your day to let this go?" She could clearly tell that he hated his job and wasn't exactly a company man.

"Howzat?"

"Could you possibly find it in your heart to give me a break? I'd be forever grateful."

He turned and noticed her for the very first time.

And stood stock-still.

His eyes focused on her face, her eyes. Her hair.

She could feel the man's darkness turning lighter. A moment later, it dimmed.

Nice, his eyes said as the beginnings of a smile touched his chubby cheeks. *Real nice…*

How is this happening to me? she wondered. *How am I hearing this at all? Auras? Thoughts? Feelings? How is this even real?*

What in heaven's name happened to me in the Enlightenment Room?

Focus, she told herself. *Try figuring this out later.*

"I'd really appreciate any break you can give me," she said softly, her eyes locked onto his.

130

He shook his head. "I can't—"

"You can do anything you wish. You're your own man, and you answer to no one." She couldn't believe she'd just said that. It didn't sound like anything she'd ever said before.

A moment later, he snapped out of it. It was as if he'd been in a trance. "Sure, lady." He tossed something heavy into the toolbox bolted to the side of the truck bed. "If you can get that cop over there to rip up that ticket…"

"Thank you *so* much…" She gave him a big smile.

"No problem."

The cop was busy scribbling out her ticket.

"Is there any way I can ask you to forget about this?" she asked, once again in a soft voice.

He didn't pause at all in his scribbling. "Sorry, lady, but once I start, it's a done deal."

"I'd *really* appreciate it if you can just let this slide…"

"No can do. You shouldn'ta been parked here all night."

"It really wasn't my fault. I wish you could give me a little leeway."

"Nope. Like I said—"

"Are you *sure* you want to do this, Officer?" Once again, she couldn't believe how she was acting. Not so very long ago, she would have just stood there and watched in frustration while the man finished writing the ticket.

131

Just yesterday, in fact, she would have done just that. But for some reason, yesterday seemed ages ago.

He suddenly stopped scribbling and turned. His small gray eyes met hers. She sensed a slew of emotions and an unusual blend of colors radiating from him.

"I'd *really* appreciate this, Officer..."

He continued watching her. After a few moments, he shut his pad and pocketed it and his pen. An awkward smile appeared on his lined face, and she could sense a small bubble of warmth coming from him. "Go 'head, lady. Don't worry about it. Just get back in your car and have a nice day."

"Thank you *so* much..."

Bryan looked totally mystified when she went back to the BMW. "What the hell did you do?" He watched both the cop and the tow truck driver getting back in their vehicles. "They're both...they're...*leaving*..."

"I just asked them if they'd cut me a break."

He gazed incredulously at her. The confusion showed clearly in his eyes. "Girl, that cop was writing you a *ticket*. Cops *never* stop once they start writing. And that tow truck driver..." He shook his head. "You didn't *bribe* them or anything, didja?"

She laughed. "As I just said, I asked them to give me a break."

"Seriously?"

"I used my really sweet voice."

132

She could sense his skepticism. But she couldn't blame him. She was wondering about all this herself. She was somehow convinced that whatever had happened to her in Margaret Freedman's Enlightenment Room had somehow made all this possible. And that she shouldn't question anything.

She chose to do just that. At least for now.

She smiled at Bryan. "Once again, thanks for everything you've done for me."

"It was a pleasure."

"I don't know if I'll ever see you again. I sincerely hope you sell the house."

"Thanks. And please take care of yourself." He shot another quick glance at the cruiser that had already pulled away. He turned back to her and smiled. "Although something tells me that's not really much of an issue with you." He waved, flicked on the ignition, backed out of his spot and eased past her.

She watched him, knowing full well that she'd lied to him.

She hoped with all her heart that he would never sell the house where the beautiful spirit lady Margaret Freedman had once lived happily for so many years.

PART 2

Chapter 15

Lynn got back to her apartment in St. Clairsville just after 8:00 that evening.

The moment she walked through the door, she realized something was very different. The fact that she felt different in her own place, among all her personal belongings, made her tremble.

Was it the apartment itself? Hardly.

It's me. I'm different...somehow...

And with that thought, she found herself staring at her reflection in the antique mirror her grandmother had left her. Lynn had hung it on the wall the day she moved in. And as she stepped closer to it, she realized that what both she and Bryan had noticed back in Margaret Freedman's house had followed her all the way home. The difference in her hair, her eyes and her face had stayed with her.

Was this a good thing? Or something she should really be worrying about?

She got out of her filthy clothes and tossed them in the laundry room. Then, while focusing on more practical matters, she stepped into her shower. As the heavy spray of warm water cascaded down upon her, she tried very hard to keep her mind from looping.

But it was rough. The incident in Wheeling with the cop and the tow truck driver had brought back the total confusion that had been plaguing her for the last several hours.

"Cops never stop once they start writing..."

She'd heard that same thing several times, and from different people. However, the cop had stopped writing the ticket the moment she'd asked him to give her a break. And the tow truck driver had, also at her request, stopped hooking up the Honda to his equipment.

All she'd done was ask them for a favor.

Was that all that had been necessary?

Why had everything changed so drastically?

She'd received a parking ticket a year earlier, when, after work, she'd parked across the street from the St. Clairsville Post Office. A few minutes after 6:30 at evening, she'd rushed inside and dropped off an envelope. She remained inside less than a minute—just long enough to slip the envelope into the slot, turn, and hurry back outside...

But by the time she'd pushed open the heavy glass door, gone back outside and approached the top step, a cop was standing beside her car, writing her a ticket.

She'd spent the next five minutes imploring him to forgive her for this minor indiscretion, promising him that she'd never do it again. But once the tall, slender man had started scribbling, he'd become a machine, ignoring her completely, his primary goal in life focused on finishing his task.

But less than an hour ago, something totally different had happened. Something she'd never experienced before—or even heard of—in her entire life.

What was going on?

Was it the fact that she looked different? Felt different?

How could her brief experience in the Enlightenment Room possibly explain this unheard-of phenomenon?

And what was it about those strange sensations she'd picked up on during her encounters with the two men? Darkness and frustration? Feelings of warmth and satisfaction?

"Nothing bad will ever happen to you again..."

Once again, that same phrase came right back, baffling her just as much this time as it had before.

Also came other sensations that seemed just as bizarre.

The strongest, of course, was why she hadn't felt any shred of anger or disappointment when she and Bryan first saw the tow truck and the police cruiser pulled up to her Honda.

The others—the feelings of warmth and brightness, not to mention the emotions emanating from both men—were just as uncertain.

Very, very strange indeed...

After her shower, she dropped her dirty clothes into the washer, added some detergent, started it up and went back to the bedroom. She put on a fresh tee shirt and jeans and slipped into the kitchen to see what she could dig up for a late supper.

Just as she opened the fridge, her cell rang. She fished through her handbag, grabbed it and picked it up.

She groaned. It was Frank again.

When she'd gotten back into the Honda after talking to the Wheeling cop, she'd reached under her seat and checked her bag to make sure everything was still there. Her phone was right where she'd left it, in the side pocket. When she'd turned it on, the screen displayed twenty-seven messages. Twenty from Frank, four from Ariana, and three from Jodi Kenner, her store assistant. She'd been much too wired right then to talk to anyone, so she'd ignored the calls, returned the cell to her bag, and concentrated on the drive back to St. Clairsville.

She just wasn't in the mood to talk to anyone right now—especially Frank. She thoroughly enjoyed the warm feelings since she'd left Margaret Freedman's house and didn't want to engage in anything that would spoil her mood.

She pulled out a dish of macaroni and cheese she'd brought home from the supermarket two days earlier. The moment she slipped it in the microwave, the cell buzzed again.

Frank again.

Knowing how stubborn the man could be, she knew he wouldn't stop calling. With a deep sigh, she picked it up and turned it on. "Yes?"

"Where the hell have you been?" The man sounded exasperated. "I've been calling and calling!"

137

She felt the brightness of her mood darkening instantly. "My voicemail says you left nearly two dozen messages."

"Why haven't you returned my calls, Lynnie?"

Her mood darkened even more. That was not the question she expected him to ask. "Is this why you're calling? To ask why I haven't called you back?"

She heard him sigh. "Where have you been? I've been out of my mind with worry!"

The moment Frank dodged her question, something popped into her head, coaxing her memory to recall him doing this very same thing dozens of other times. Then she wondered why she hadn't noticed this before now.

Her mood darkened yet again when something else came to her. Most people would act the way he was acting because of genuine concern. This made her realize Frank wasn't your average person. She was quite certain he'd dodged her question simply because he was attempting to lay some guilt on her for not returning his calls.

She noticed something else about him she hadn't thought much about before. The man seemed comfortable—almost happy—when he was spreading around some guilt, especially when he'd done something he wasn't proud of. And since he obviously felt guilty about his indiscretion with Adriana, he no doubt wanted Lynn to feel some culpability herself.

But despite these negative feelings, she sensed a gathering of bright emotions caressing her. She knew she had to hold onto them. But to do this, she had to keep him away from her.

"I really don't want to talk right now, Frank…"

"Baby, I can understand why you're so upset with me…"

"Then this should tell you why I don't want to talk to you right now."

"We *need* to talk. We need to put this thing behind us."

"*Behind* us?" That was the worst possible statement he could have made. "You honestly think you can put this *thing*—as you so crudely termed it—*behind* us?"

His sudden silence told her she'd struck a nerve. It made her feel a little better.

"Well?"

"Baby, I know I messed up—"

"You did more than that, Frank."

He was actually feeling some remorse. She could hear it in his voice. "I know, baby. I also know that there can be no reasonable excuse for what I've done. But if you'll just give me a few minutes to explain my side of it—"

"Your side of it is the same as Ariana's. You had sex with her. She had sex with you. Cased closed, in my book."

"But if you'll just—"

"I told you I didn't want to talk right now. And I mean it. I really and truly *mean* it!" She rubbed the back of her neck. She was struggling to keep calm, to hold on to the brightness. But each moment talking with him brought back more shades of that dreaded darkness.

"All right. We won't talk about that. But will you please tell me where you've been since you stormed out of my place? I was sick with worry. When you walked out...when you left...I called your parents. They hadn't heard from you. I called the shop this morning, but Jodi hadn't seen you. I really thought something horrible had happened to you."

"I drove to Wheeling, Frank. Seeing you naked with my sister upset me so much, I had to get away. I hope you realize that. I should hope you'd understand how much you really hurt me."

"I do realize that, and I really wish I could do something to—"

"I drove to Wheeling and stopped at the first bar I came to."

Silence.

"I had one drink and decided to come back home, but two very large drunken hicks from Bridgeport grabbed me off the street and forced me into their pickup."

"My *God*, Lynn! Are you all right? Did they...what the hell did they—"

"They took me to their place a few miles south of Bridgeport, way out in the sticks. They started feeding me their homemade hooch to get me drunk. They were going to take me to their house and have whole bunches of sadistic fun with me in what they called their Playroom."

A heavy silence. She could hear him breathing harder. This made her feel even better.

But it also made the warmth inside her turn cold.

"Wh-What happened, Lynn?" His voice sounded weak. "Did they...I mean, were you able to...what the hell did you do?"

She decided to let his imagination work on him a little, so she didn't reply right off. After about half a minute, she said, "I got away before they could do anything."

"Good Lord." A heavy sigh. "I'm *so* glad. If I'd known anything like that would have—"

"'Bye, Frank." She hung up. Then she went back to heating up the mac and cheese.

The cell buzzed once again, but she ignored it.

Later, as she sat on the living room couch, eating her dinner and drinking port wine, her old recording of Beethoven's 7th Symphony, which she hadn't played since high school, radiated brilliantly from her stereo in a corner of the room.

Once she'd finished her dinner, she relaxed on the couch, closed her eyes and let the beautiful music caress her.

She thought it very strange that Beethoven's music could so easily bring back the brightness in a giant wave of soft, sensuous warmth, sending the darkness scurrying away...

Chapter 16

At 11:00, Lynn decided to call it a night.

She was extremely tired, and since the shop was closed on Sunday, she figured she owed it to herself to spend the day on the couch, listening to music, watching a movie, and finishing the tub of cherry vanilla ice cream she'd bought a week earlier.

Being lazy sounded wonderful. A full day of doing absolutely nothing could be just what she needed for a recharge. She'd call Jodi in the morning and let her know she was all right and would be in bright and early on Monday morning. But she didn't want to do anything—or speak with anyone—that would bring back the darkness or any sort of negative energy. A full twenty-four hours of complete rest sounded ideal. She'd be totally refreshed and ready to resume her life.

However, just as she was about to turn off the living room lamp, the doorbell buzzed.

Frowning, she shuffled over to the door and squinted at the peephole. And groaned.

It was Frank.

Sighing deeply, she struggled to keep the anger at bay. She didn't want to see Frank right now. Judging by how she felt, she probably wouldn't want to see him ever again. And she was much too drained to engage in what would turn into a heated argument in no time at all. She'd loved Frank Alden and wanted to spend the rest of her life with him...

But what he'd done was something no woman with any ounce of self-respect could forgive or forget. She wasn't about to lower her guard. And she certainly didn't want to answer the door.

Another buzz.

"Lynnie? *Please* let me in!"

She stood frozen in the foyer, her hands clenched into fists, those last few bits of bright emotions clinging desperately to her. She feared that if she opened the door, the brightness would dim, and the darkness would shove its way inside and take over right away.

She didn't want the darkness to return. She'd never liked the darkness. Darkness was cold. And frightening. All sorts of evil, nasty things lived there. Things she never wanted to see—or feel—ever again.

She loved the light. Light was wonderful. Its warmth, its comfort. Things were *so* much better in the light. Happier. Nothing to fear. And life was much sweeter.

"Lynnie!"

He wasn't going away. Despite her reluctance to open the door, she knew full well that the man would stay there and continue being a nuisance until she let him have his way.

But what could he possibly say that would change anything? What could Frank Alden tell her that would justify what he'd done? How could anything that came out of the arrogant jerk's mouth change what had happened?

He couldn't very well turn back the clock, could he? No one could. He couldn't possibly undo what he and Ariana had done.

The doorbell buzzed again, three quick times in succession.

She forced both hands through her hair and tried once again to ignore the growing anger. He wasn't going anywhere. She'd known him since college. One of his most dominant traits was his stubbornness. He'd stand out there on the front stoop until she opened the door, or one of her neighbors called the cops on him for being a nuisance. It was strange that she'd always considered this trait one of the qualities that had attracted her the most. In business, stubbornness was a much sought-after commodity. But now, all she could think of was how irritating he was. How he was grating on her last nerve. And how the love she'd once had for him had dissolved so quickly.

She had only one of two choices. She could ignore him and go to bed. And leave him out there, bringing attention to himself. Or she could open the door, invite him in and listen to his nonsense until she decided she'd had enough.

That second option seemed more practical. His was the last face she wanted to see, so why not make this truly memorable? Why not let him in and watch him squirm and sweat and stutter his way out of this? It might be just what she needed for some quality entertainment before she went to bed. And, as an added bonus, his nonsense might even bore her so much that she'd be able to sleep better.

Sighing tiredly, she unlocked the door and pulled it open. And hoped with all her heart that her inner warmth would remain right where it was.

Frank stood on the front stoop in his charcoal-gray sweatshirt and jeans, looking pitiful. His red-blond hair, always perfectly groomed, was unkempt. His cheeks, always freshly shaven, had darkened with twenty-four-hour stubble. He looked like someone who had just been caught doing something despicable and feared he was about to pay the price.

She had the strong feeling karma had somehow swooped in to complete this fitting picture of proper comeuppance.

"May I come in?"

"Why not? Don't want the neighbors complaining, do we?" She backed up and watched him struggle to maintain his dignity. Head lowered, he shuffled in, closed the door, and turned slowly to face her. Waiting for a special invitation, obviously.

She continued standing there in silence, her expression as blank as she could manage.

"Well? Aren't you gonna invite me in?"

"You're already in."

He sighed. "Lynn, can you *please* be civilized for just a few moments?"

She couldn't believe what he'd just said. She felt some brightness drifting away. "You're talking about *me* being civilized?"

"I just think you're acting a little—"

"Angry? Short? Abrupt? Nasty? That sort of thing?"

He seemed to shrink a little at each word.

"Frank, you spent yesterday afternoon in your bed with my sister. It happens to be the same bed you and I used to share. The same bed we'd been sharing for the last couple of years. The same bed where you and I expressed our feelings, our emotions, for one another. And now you're actually asking *me* to be civilized?" More brightness broke away. A fresh trickle of hot anger swooped in, settling between her shoulder blades.

He remained silent, avoiding her stare. A few moments later, he began fidgeting. She could tell he was struggling for something to say that wouldn't anger her further. "Can we please talk in the living room?"

She didn't move. She didn't want him in her living room, didn't want him in her apartment at all...but right now, she didn't seem to have much choice.

"Just give me a minute, all right? Please?"

She watched him and considered her options. One last stab at clinging to whatever light was left helped her push the anger away.

"Nothing bad will ever happen to you again..."

Despite the circumstances, that phrase still lingered somewhere in her mind.

She took a breath, turned and went into the living room.

He followed her in and stood in the doorway, looking lost.

She sat down in the chair and gestured to the couch facing her. She'd chosen the chair so he wouldn't sit too close. She couldn't bear him being

146

close to her right now. Or touching him. Or even smelling his aftershave, or the whiskey on his breath. The very thought of any closeness with him made her nauseous. The fact that he was even here in the first place angered her enough.

He came in and sat.

"Just why are you here, Frank?" She saw no reason to drag this out. She longed to end this meeting as quickly as possible. She desperately wanted the brightness to come back and feared the darkness would remain as long as Frank was here.

He didn't reply right off. After a few moments, he took a deep breath. "Would you mind if I had a drink? I could really use something…something to settle my—"

"Haven't you had enough already?"

"Lynn, please. This is rough for me."

She wanted to tell him that this *should* be rough. And that forgiveness on her part was not exactly in the cards right now. But that would most likely start another argument. "Go right ahead. Have your drink. Say what you came to say." The moment she'd said it, the light came back, and she could feel at least some of the anger slinking away.

He hurried over to the drink tray, where she kept his single malt Scotch, three small bottles of vodka, and several bottles of tonic, when she wanted a drink after work. There was also some brandy and rum her old college friends enjoyed whenever they came over from Pittsburgh for an occasional visit.

147

He poured a large drink from one of the glasses on the tray. "Want something?"

"No." She wanted him to state his business as quickly as possible and leave. She'd become slightly less tired and wondered if it had something to do with the anger going away and the brightness rushing back. Whatever it was, she knew it would not be permanent. Frank had come here to defend his actions. Of that, she was certain. He would no doubt say something ridiculous. Justifying his actions had been his nature ever since she'd known him. She just hoped she could send him on his way before more damage could be done.

"You're sure?" He was reaching for the vodka bottle.

"I'm good. Really. In fact, I was heading off to bed when you came."

The suggestion obviously hadn't done what she'd hoped. Instead of apologizing for the late hour, he merely sipped from the glass and came right back. He sat and began staring at her.

"Something wrong?"

It took him several moments to reply. He was squinting. "You look…different."

She remembered her exchange with Bryan Grant and was afraid this same thing would happen now, which could prolong Frank's stay. "Maybe it's because I don't want you to be here. Or because you're here when I want to get into bed and sleep."

"No. It's not that at all."

"Frank…"

"I really don't know what's different. Your hair, maybe?"

She was in no mood for this. "What exactly do you want, Frank? It *is* late, you know…"

He had another swig of Scotch. His gaze never left her.

"Talk, Frank. I'd really like to go to bed. It's been a terribly long day."

"You're *really* all right? I mean, you're not hurt, are you? I'm talking about those two punks in Wheeling—"

"As I told you, I was able to get away from them. You didn't forget, did you? You were listening, weren't you?"

"I remember. And yes. Of *course* I was listening."

"So then, to repeat what I already told you, I got away before they could do anything really bad to me."

"Where'd you go? I mean, how did you get back to Wheeling? You were gone more than—"

"Get to the point, Frank."

He had another sip of Scotch and put his half-empty glass on the table. "Baby, I really think we should pursue this…this Wheeling thing. We're talking unlawful imprisonment, kidnapping, attempted rape, possible battery, all kinds of emotional distress—"

"They were morons. And they were drunk. They probably don't even remember what happened." She didn't want him getting into this. It would most definitely make this situation worse.

And it really wasn't the most important issue right now.

He shrugged. "They're grown men, aren't they?"

"What does that have to do with anything?"

"Grown men are supposed to be responsible for their own actions. In the eyes of the law, anyone over the age of—"

"As I just said, they were drunk."

"Even so, I don't think we should let them get away with this."

"They probably slept it off and don't even remember me or what they did." She saw no reason for him to go on about this. She had to force him back onto matters he was ignoring, obviously to get her mind away from the most crucial issue. She decided to tell him a lie that would end this discussion. "They went home after I got away from them."

He went silent, sipping his Scotch. "Listen...I've got a lawyer friend, Bill Taylor, and if I—"

"I know all about Bill Taylor." She shook her head. He was not getting the message at all.

"Then you must know he's a real badass in the courtroom."

She really wanted him to leave. He was using everything he could think of to skirt around the real reason for his visit. Talking about this postponed facing the inevitable.

"I'm *not* going to pursue this, Frank." She sensed the brightness of her aura returning to

150

replace the darkness she had desperately tried pushing away.

"But why not? Actually—" Then he stopped and stared at her.

"Actually, *what*?"

Silently he raised his glass and brought it to his lips, studying her while he drank.

"Frank?"

Still watching her, he lowered the glass very slowly. "It really *is* your hair, Lynnie…"

She sighed tiredly. "What about my hair?"

"I noticed something before, but now…now that I've seen it in the light… It's…it's absolutely gorgeous…"

The brightness had obviously returned. And when she considered his reaction, she almost laughed. "You sound surprised."

"Well, yes…no…it's just that…" He sighed. "I just can't get over how *good* you look…"

"Should I take that as a compliment? Or is this just some other ruse to distract me?"

He began squinting again. She wondered why he hadn't brought along his glasses. "Your face…seems different, too…" He tilted his head. "Are you wearing contacts?"

"No…"

"Your eyes…they look larger, darker…almost an emerald green."

"It's the lighting."

"They seem so *different*…"

"It's the Scotch. You're—"

"No. *Not* the damned Scotch." He shook his head. "It's *you*, Lynnie. Something's happened to you, and it's the damnedest thing I ever saw."

"A couple of things happened to me, Frank."

He sipped more Scotch and stared at his glass as he lowered it. She supposed he was considering what she'd just said. "I...wasn't talking about that."

"Then what is it?" She felt the darkness coming back.

"As I said before, it's you. Your looks. You're absolutely stunning. In fact, I'd swear that, in this light, you're just as beautiful and as sexy as your sister."

It was the worst thing he could have said. She had to close her eyes and clench her jaw to get through the next few tense moments.

Another wave of darkness swept through her, heavier and thicker than ever before.

And when she finally opened her eyes, she realized she'd gotten up from her chair. And had crossed the living room. And was now back in the foyer, pointing rather shakily to the door. "Get out, Frank."

He gawked stupidly at her.

"I mean it. Get out of my apartment."

"But Lynnie—"

"I'm not gonna tell you again."

He slowly rose from the chair. He stood, shaking a little. "Baby, I really didn't mean anything that would—"

"I know exactly what you meant." It took her a moment to remember what he'd said, but it finally came back, and with it, the rage. "Now get out."

"But—"

"Now."

He held out his hands. He seemed to be surrendering.

"This instant."

"Baby, I'm really very, *very* sorry—"

"I know you are, Frank. You really *are* sorry, and I want you to—" She stopped just then and thought about what she should say. The darkness had taken hold, but it occurred to her that if she kept her composure, she just might be able to get through this. The Wheeling cop and the tow truck driver entered her thoughts at that moment. *Soft voice*, her thoughts said. *Soft. Unthreatening. Gentle.* Use your "good" voice, just as you did with them, and this just might turn out okay. Maybe the warmth and the brightness will come back.

Taking a breath, she said very softly, "Please leave, Frank, and I'd appreciate it if you never came back."

"That's *cold,* Lynnie..."

"I'm sorry, but there really isn't much to say anymore, is there?" *Keep it soft, gentle...* "You can leave right now. I really don't want to get angry. I'm much too tired."

"But—"

"Now, Frank."

Looking sheepish, he started to say something else.

She felt the darkness dimming slightly but knew that if she didn't keep things soft and gentle, it would come right back. "If you don't leave right now, I'm calling the police. They'll get here in just a few minutes and arrest you. I really don't want you here." Despite her intentions, she felt the anger taking hold again. She took another breath, but it didn't seem to improve things. The anger—as well as the hurt—just would not leave.

"Lynnie—"

"*Now*, Frank!"

Without another word, he turned and shuffled out of the room.

She waited until he'd closed the door behind him. Then she turned off the light and went to the door to put on the chain. Still shaking, she took a deep breath and closed her eyes. *Good thoughts. Brightness. Warmth.* It took a minute or so for the heat to ebb. Finally, feeling slightly less upset, she went down the hall, where her bedroom eagerly awaited her.

A moment later, the high-pitched screeching of brakes echoed outside. The loud thud that followed made the front wall vibrate.

Chapter 17

Frank lay on the pavement near the curb, his blood-stained face facing the thick metal base of the streetlamp.

The silver van that had slammed into him had stopped a few yards straight ahead, at the four-way light. The driver, a large, dark-haired young man, stood in the middle of the street, trembling while gazing wide-eyed at Frank.

A police car had already shown up. The officer parked his vehicle a few yards from Frank and placed half a dozen red cones behind and in front of the squad car. Since it was nearly midnight, there was little traffic. The few vehicles crept by slowly, drivers and passengers gawking at the sight.

Her heart thumping frantically, Lynn walked over to the curb and gazed numbly at the man she'd once loved. The man who just the day before had engaged in an afternoon of sex with her sister. The same man who just a few minutes earlier had come into her home and tried smoothing over what he'd done.

The man who now lay there, dead.

I did this, she told herself as the panic swept through her. *I was responsible for this*.

But how? How could she think she'd caused this horrible accident?

She'd told this man to leave her house. He'd betrayed their trust and she didn't want to have anything to do with him again.

That was it.

Well, *wasn't* it?

Her angry words came right back, filling her head with the same anger and darkness that had heated her up just minutes earlier.

"Please leave, Frank...and never came back..."

But what did that have to do with—

No. She refused to believe she'd caused this.

What made her think she could have caused someone to kill himself after leaving her apartment? What made her think anyone could do something like that?

No one in the world possessed that much power.

This was random. A simple accident—nothing else. Frank was upset. He wasn't thinking clearly. He'd left the house and was so angry, hurt and confused by what she'd said to him that he wasn't watching where he was going. He'd crossed the street and wasn't even aware of where he was. He didn't even realize that a vehicle was right there the moment before it slammed into him.

But she just couldn't ignore the obvious. She couldn't dismiss what had just happened between them in her apartment.

I told him to leave, and he'd done just that. He'd left my apartment, crossed the street, and was run down.

She stood less than five feet from the curb, gazing numbly at him and forcing herself not to scream. Wanting him to get back up and walk away. To start breathing again. Maybe he'd even smile at her, then apologize for what he'd done. She wanted to take this nightmare back maybe just five or ten minutes, back in her apartment, a moment or two before he'd made that last hurtful remark.

But she couldn't. She was painfully aware that she couldn't. No one could.

She shivered, and an instant later, realized that the brightness had left her. It had gone away. Just like that. The darkness was back in full force, and she feared that it was there to stay.

She didn't want the darkness clinging to her. She wanted the brightness to come back. The brightness and the warmth. The happy thoughts and the feelings that made her look and feel so much better. The illusion that life was wonderful. That she was truly happy. That she'd finally become the beautiful, stunning woman she'd always wanted to be.

She closed her eyes and willed the brightness to come back. To forget what had just happened. *Please come back. Please stay with me. I didn't mean this. I didn't mean any of this at all!*

The darkness remained, closing tightly around her. She shivered and wrapped her arms around herself. Maybe she could squeeze the darkness away. If she could rid herself of it, the brightness could sneak back and take over again.

Squeeze it away. Tighter, tighter…

The darkness didn't budge.

The sudden realization made her cringe. She knew right then why Margaret Freedman had taken her into the Enlightenment Room. After all, they

157

were kindred spirits, weren't they? The spirit lady wanted to share things with Lynn that she didn't want to share with anyone else. Lynn could now remember the warmth, the brightness, the happy emotions. And, more importantly, Margaret telling her things she needed to know, things she should always keep with her. Things that would enable her to live a wonderfully happy life.

"Nothing bad will ever—"

The rest of that wonderful, loving phrase was gone. She'd let her emotions turn dark and cold. And as a result, everything good, bright, and wonderful had abandoned her.

No. I can't let it all go. I just can't!

She closed her eyes once again and willed the brightness to come back. And stay with her. Forever.

Please come back. Please! I never intended this to happen. Never in my wildest dreams would I ever wish someone dead.

The darkness remained, pressing coldly against her.

"Miss?" A strange voice. Someone was trying to get her attention.

Startled, she opened her eyes and looked up at the man dressed in a blue uniform. He was tall and broad-shouldered and, judging by his solemn expression, very concerned.

"Are you all right, miss?"

She gazed at him and realized she could not speak. Her mind had gone blank, and all she could focus on was the man's face. There was a large dark mole on his left cheek. She also saw a small white scar just above his cheekbone, very close to his eye. His eyes were dark and somewhat blood-shot. She wondered if he was getting enough sleep. She'd seen him once or twice before. This was not unusual, since St. Clairsville was a small city, with a small police force, as well. She guessed he was a nice man, and his concern for her showed greatly in his eyes. This touched her. You didn't see much concern in people anymore—especially with the younger crowd, kids wandering aimlessly down the street, totally engrossed in their cell phones and iPads. Texting and sexting one another while ignoring the rest of the—

"Miss?" The man sounded even more anxious. "Did you see what happened here?"

She continued staring and found that her eyes had glazed over. The man facing her had faded, and a few moments later, blended into two separate images.

Snap out of it, girl!

She closed her eyes and shook herself, and when she opened them, she noticed that he'd turned right back into one person. But he still looked worried. He'd just asked her a question and was waiting for an answer. The problem was that she couldn't remember what he'd asked.

He probably wanted to know if she saw what happened.

Yes. This seemed the sort of question a cop would ask. And she should tell him. After all, she was the reason this happened in the first place, right? She'd told Frank to leave her apartment and never come back. She was angry at him and hurt for his horrible indiscretion, and she couldn't forgive him for that.

Yes, Officer. I know all about what happened. In fact, I was the reason this happened in the first place. I told this man to leave my home. Well, he walked out the door and was promptly run down by that van over there. Strange—don't you think?

Then what?

Should she just stand here patiently and wait while he radioed for the loony wagon to rush right over, scoop her up with a butterfly net and drive her to the nearest mental institution?

Or should she just try and think this through so she could tell him what happened?

What *did* happen?

"Get out, Frank..."

Is this when the darkness first slammed through her? Is this when it overwhelmed her, absorbing every single thought in her brain, and pushing the hatred into her spirit? Is this when she stopped thinking altogether and surrendered her thoughts to the frightening blackness flashing before her eyes?

"Miss?"

"He came to see me earlier," she heard herself saying.

"Where do you live, miss?"

She pointed.

He jotted something down in his notebook. It was thick, with a black leather cover, and the pen he

160

was using was a ballpoint. The pad looked very similar to the one the Wheeling cop had used.

Why hadn't she noticed it before?

Perhaps it was because she'd been so totally focused on his face. His worried look. The mole. And, of course, the scar. She couldn't help wondering how he'd gotten it. But she knew this wasn't exactly the right time to ask.

"Is that what he was doing? Leaving your place?"

She nodded.

He wrote something else down.

"His name was Frank," she said softly. "Frank Alden. He was thirty-eight, lived just a few blocks from here, and managed his own Hedge Fund account—"

"I know about the man, miss." He kept scribbling.

She should have suspected. Everyone in town knew Frank, so it was really no surprise.

"We'd been seeing one another for quite a while." She knew that it no longer mattered but felt she should tell the cop. It somehow made this more personal—at least, to her. It would make it clearer why Frank was here at this time of the night, why he'd been crossing the street. Why he'd been preoccupied and hadn't noticed the van.

But it didn't make it less painful.

"I'm sorry, miss."

"Pardon me?"

He looked up from his notebook. "I'm sorry this happened."

"Thank you." That was sweet of him. She'd never thought police officers were sweet--or even had feelings. Perhaps this was because she hadn't really known any of them very well. And the cop who had given her the ticket last year hadn't demonstrated much kindness at all.

But that was a different matter entirely.

The Wheeling cop she'd seen just a few hours earlier had clearly demonstrated some serious kindness. Well, hadn't he? That should change her opinion, shouldn't it?

"If you'll just give me a few details about yourself, you can go back home, and we won't bother you any longer."

"Details?"

"Your name, address. The nature of the visit of the deceased."

The deceased. That meant Frank. It also meant he was dead. The very utterance of that word by a stranger made her queasy.

My God. How could this have happened to me? How could I have let it happen? Frank's dead, and it's because of me—I know it is. How will I be able to live with myself? How will I be able to accept this?

"Miss?"

She'd forgotten what she was supposed to tell him. "Yes?"

"Your name? Address?" He shrugged. "The nature of Mr. Alden's visit?"

162

"Oh. Yes. I'm sorry." Taking a deep breath, she forced herself to focus and was finally able to give him the details he needed.

Then, just as the medical unit eased to a stop less than twenty feet from where Frank lay, she turned her back on the nightmare and trudged up the grassy knoll leading to her apartment.

She went back inside, closed the door, hurried down the hall, went into the bathroom, bent over the toilet, and threw up.

A few minutes later, after dabbing her face with a cold washcloth, she killed the horrible taste in her mouth with mint mouthwash. Then, avoiding the mirror, she went back into the living room and collapsed on the couch.

She spent the next hour staring at the blank TV screen while struggling even harder to bring the brightness back.

The darkness caressing her grew even heavier.

Chapter 18

The next morning, Lynn awoke and discovered she'd spent the night on the living room couch.

Once her mind cleared, and her memory went back to the previous night, a series of horrifying images flashed by, making her nauseous.

Frank was dead. He'd come to see her and when she told him to leave, he left the apartment and was killed by a passing van.

And it was her fault.

Well, wasn't it?

Hadn't she told him to leave? Wasn't he run down once he'd left? Hadn't she *wanted* him to die?

No. I did not *want him to die.*

Are you sure? that cursed inner voice asked.

Of course I'm sure. I loved Frank and even planned to marry him one day. I'd never want him to die. Yes, he had sex with Ariana, and yes, they hurt me very, very deeply. And because of that hurt, that betrayal, I no longer wanted him in my life.

But that did not *mean I wanted him dead. And if I knew even for a single moment that he'd be run down just seconds after he walked out the front door, I would never have insisted that he leave in the first place.*

Are you certain that's what you were thinking? the inner voice asked once again.

Yes, I'm certain. I'd never deliberately wish anyone *to be run down in the street. Especially Frank. Especially someone I once loved.*

164

You weren't angry with him when he left? You weren't enraged? You weren't seriously hurt?

Yes, I was angry. I was enraged. And hurt. After all, he'd committed the most unforgiveable sin possible. But I'm not the kind of person who would wish someone dead. I've never been that sort of person—never!

You're certain you weren't angry enough in that one single moment to wish him dead?

No. She wasn't sure. She wasn't sure for the simple reason that Frank had ruined everything—their life together, their future together—by committing that one single act of outright stupidity.

But that still didn't mean she wanted him dead, did it?

Well? Did it?

Hadn't she *wanted* something bad to happen to him? Hadn't she thought about it?

And it had happened, hadn't it?

Frank was dead. But she hadn't *caused* it, had she? Believing so would go against every single mode of logic she could think of. As she told herself the night before, while standing outside, staring at his lifeless body lying near the curb, Frank had been upset. He hadn't been thinking clearly. And as a result, he wasn't looking where he was going. He'd been so torn up and frustrated by her anger –and by her rejection of him—that he simply wasn't aware of what he was doing.

"It's not my fault," she told the living room, hoping her voice would convince her of what she'd just said. "It couldn't possibly be. I'm not someone with frightening superpowers. I simply can't suggest something and make it happen. This was chance. Nothing else. Frank just wasn't paying attention to where he was going."

Struggling to rid her mind of such nonsense, she got up and went into the kitchen to make coffee. She had a full day to pull herself together before she went back to the store. Right now, she needed a shower and something to put in her stomach. Then she could listen to more beautiful music from her stereo and maybe put on an old movie later on. She needed to try very hard to relax and empty her mind of what she thought had happened last night. Otherwise, she'd go mad.

One thing was certain: she had to stop blaming herself for Frank's death. To do that, she had to stop thinking that she had special powers. And she had to force herself to remember what she'd believed most of her life—that most everything that happened in life was random, and that many of those things were simply accidental.

The issue with the Wheeling cop and the tow truck operator were separate instances altogether. The cop could have been having a really terrific day; he might have wanted to spread his cheer with someone who needed a helping hand. And, judging by his attitude, she truly believed the tow truck operator didn't like his job or who he was working for. Refusing to tow her Honda could have been some sort of revenge thing for him.

Frank was dead simply because he was careless and much too distracted to look where he was going. He wasn't dead because of anything she'd done. Or wished. Or suggested.

That sounded logical, didn't it?

She hoped she could convince herself she was right about all this.

Because right now, she just couldn't get any of this out of her mind. She just couldn't believe that her power of suggestion might not have been strong enough to make the horror come true.

Chapter 19

Jodi was already at the shop by the time Lynn arrived shortly before nine the next morning.

Jodi looked like she hadn't slept very well. Her long reddish-brown hair, which normally hung halfway to her waist, was tied with a black rope in a thick ponytail. It obviously hadn't been washed, and her large light-blue eyes were blood-shot.

Jodi followed Lynn into the office and grabbed a Kleenex from the box on the desk. It was clear that the word was out and that most everyone had heard what happened. In an area the size of St. Clairsville, any sort of news spread like wildfire.

"You've obviously heard about Frank," Lynn said.

"I'm *so* sorry, sweetie." Jodi rushed right over and hugged her. Lynn let the girl do her thing. Jodi was a sweet girl and a notorious hugger. She was also very emotional, crying at the drop of a hat.

Lynn thought it strange that Jodi's habit hadn't bothered her before. But now she found that she was uncomfortable with this unexpected show of emotion and didn't experience any relief until the girl pulled away.

"Is there anything I can do?" Jodi wiped her eyes carefully with the tissue. Her eyeliner had already smeared.

"I'm all right. Thanks." Lynn slipped past her, opened the bottom desk drawer, and laid her handbag inside. She closed the drawer and straightened. Jodi was still standing there, gazing wide-eyed at her. The girl was obviously deeply stunned by the tragic news.

"Let's open up." Lynn wanted more than ever to start the workday.

Jodi nodded, turned, and led the way back out into the store.

As Lynn went over to unlock the front door, Jodi said, "Have you heard from Frank's folks yet?"

"No..." Lynn stopped what she was doing. She hadn't even thought of Frank's family. Although Frank's parents were divorced, he'd always made great pains to stay in contact with both of them. His mother had remarried and had been living in the South Hills area of Pittsburgh. His father, a CPA, lived with his third wife in Ligonier. Lynn had only talked to them a couple of times. They'd both been somewhat uncomfortable in her presence but had always treated her cordially. However, she suspected that when she saw them this time, the encounter would be far from pleasant.

"You didn't call them? When it happened?"

Lynn unlocked the front door, flipped the CLOSED sign to OPEN, then went over to straighten out one of the displays. "I didn't even think of it, actually. I don't know why, but I turned kind of numb. I even slept on the couch after it hap...when I came back inside after...after the accident."

"You were in shock. And I can't say as I blame you one bit."

169

Lynn stepped back from her work and thought about that for a moment. Yes. Jodi was probably right. What else could it have been?

She knew exactly what it was. It might have indeed been shock, but it wasn't exactly what Jodi was talking about.

"I don't even know why you came in this morning." Jodi went over to the register, picked up a stack of printed shop cards and sorted through them. "With what you've just been through?" She shook her head.

"I'm okay. Really." Lynn didn't want to go through this with anyone. Since Jodi had brought it up, Lynn thought about her future encounter with Frank's parents and knew she didn't want to face them at all. They'd have all sorts of questions she wouldn't want to answer. They might even get nasty if they didn't like her answers. Especially Frank's father, who'd been a Marine in Vietnam and tended to be abrasive when dealing with people. And if the encounter went particularly badly, Lynn was certain she wouldn't be able to end things on a positive note.

But she probably wouldn't have much choice.

"How can you possibly be okay?" Jodi asked. "You and Frank were close. At least, that's how it looked to—"

"We were having problems." Lynn was growing weary of all this and wanted it to end. Talking about it had brought back the guilt, and she feared she wouldn't be able to handle much more of it without saying something that would hurt Jodi's

170

feelings. Hurting Jodi was a lot like kicking a baby dog.

She took a deep breath and struggled to push away the cold darkness smothering her.

"Really?" Jodi was obviously confused. "*Serious* problems?"

"I'd say so."

Jodi waited for more of an explanation. When Lynn didn't elaborate, Jodi turned back to the register.

"We were having commitment issues." Lynn decided to add something that would satisfy her friend's curiosity—at least for now. She thought that if she told her something sensitive and vague, it might suffice. It might also explain why Lynn wasn't as broken up about Frank's death as Jodi thought she should have been.

"I'm so sorry, honey. I...I guess I didn't know."

"We...didn't want to tell anyone until...until we decided to figure out what was going to work for us."

That seemed to suffice. But as soon as Lynn turned away from the front door, Jodi came closer and lowered her voice. "Can you tell me which of you was having the issue? Or is that too personal?"

Lynn sighed. Cursing herself for going this route, she said, "We both decided that we just might be moving along a little too fast, and—"

"I thought you'd both decided you'd be getting engaged. I distinctly remembered the two of you being inseparable at our Christmas party. I guess I might be remembering it wrong, but—"

"Well, both Frank and I had been drinking quite a bit that evening."

"But I honestly don't remember you telling me anything to the contrary—"

"There were complications." Lynn went back into the office, sat down at the desk, and logged onto her computer. Thankfully, Jodi had decided not to continue the questions. Lynn sighed and began to really enjoy the welcomed silence.

Moments later, the blessed silence ended. The cowbell at the front door clanged, announcing their first visitor of the day.

Lynn sighed in relief. If things went as they should, Jodi would be distracted with the customer and wouldn't want to continue to talk more about Frank for at least a little while.

But just as she logged into the shop's site to check their account, Jodi stuck her face in the doorway. "It's Ariana, honey. She'd like to see ya right away."

***

Ariana shuffled unsteadily into the office.

Lynn closed the door, turned, and gazed at her sister, who stood there in tense silence, staring at the floor. Adriana's large emerald-green eyes were moist and blood-shot. She'd obviously been crying. However, her sadness—and, undoubtedly, her guilt—didn't diminish the overall effect of her outfit. Her tailored gray business suit—perfect for her job as legal secretary for one of St. Clairsville's

172

most successful lawyers—accentuated her slimness. Her thick, flowing dark-brown hair hung in generous swirls. Her tan leather boots, with four-inch heels that made her nearly six feet tall, complemented the outfit.

Ariana was the last person Lynn wanted to see. Her striking appearance had always caused Lynn to feel both inferior and dissatisfied with her own looks. But now, Lynn realized that Ariana's presence had taken on a much different role, serving as a grim reminder of what had happened just three days ago. The very moment that disturbing realization hit her, Lynn felt a cold swell of darkness drifting dangerously close.

"Oh, Lynnie..." With a heavy sob, Ariana rushed forward, wrapping her arms around Lynn. "I'm *so* sorry! I can't believe he's...I can't...I just can't get over how totally awful this is!"

Lynn waited patiently for her sister to end her little drama, which would no doubt result in a pathetic display of self-pity. She could feel the darkness growing thicker and heavier and knew she'd have to be extra careful to hold her temper. She was still struggling with the stressful possibility that she might have been responsible for Frank's death and didn't want to take the chance that she might be right. With this in mind, she waited nervously for Ariana's sobbing to subside. And turned away the instant she felt her sister's arms releasing their hold on her.

"Why'd you come here, Ariana?" She went over to the desk and sat down. "Is this about Frank?"

Ariana sniffed, gently blotting her wet eyes with a wadded-up Kleenex. "Of course. I figured you'd need company—"

"Is this *all* you wanted to talk about?"

Ariana stared at Lynn for a few awkward moments, then took a seat facing the desk. "Sis, I really don't think this is the right time for—"

"For what? Talking about that pesky little detail of you and my boyfriend having sex just the other day?"

Ariana shook her head. Some of her hair fell in front of her face. She nudged it away with her usual flick of the wrist and applied the Kleenex lightly to her cheekbones.

"That *was* you, wasn't it?" Lynn knew she should ease up, but the images shooting past fed the anger. When she sensed the darkness moving in, she felt strangely powerless. But she'd come this far. "I'd hate to blame you for something awful and unforgivable—especially if that wasn't really you I saw when I walked in."

Ariana blotted her cheekbone while pouting. "It was me and you know it."

"So why don't you want to talk about it right now?"

"I honestly don't think this is the right time for that."

"When exactly will the right time be? At Frank's funeral? How about while we're at the cemetery, tossing flowers at his casket?"

"You're just being cruel, now…"

Yes. She was indeed being cruel. And she had no idea why. She'd just reminded herself that she should be careful. She didn't want her anger to get out of hand again. The last time she'd let go, Frank had died. She'd tried being careful, but he died anyway. And even though she wasn't one hundred percent certain what had happened, she didn't want to take any chances with her sister, even though Ariana had been pressing the wrong buttons since she came into the room.

So why am I being so vicious?

Another wave of anger whipped through her, and she took a breath and tried calming herself. *Gentle. Warm. Let the brightness in.* After another breath, she said softly, "I'm sorry, Ari. I didn't mean to come off sounding that way."

Ariana sighed. "I really can't blame you, Sis. After all, your boyfriend just died. You're entitled to be upset."

Despite her efforts, she cringed as a burst of heat shot up her spine. *Frank just died, and my sister thinks it's okay that I'm upset…*

She'd never realized just how idiotic her sister really was. She'd known all about the girl's deceptive naivete, her calculated slyness and the countless ways when, even as a child, she could manipulate men. Lynn knew that her sister was much smarter than she appeared. She just hadn't

175

fully realized how foolish the girl acted at times, which right at the moment had become utterly intolerable.

She closed her eyes and prayed that this present surge of anger would subside.

But it stayed right there, situated uncomfortably in the back of her neck.

Just don't let the darkness take over this time…

Taking another deep breath, she struggled to bring back the light. *Gentle. Soft. Brightness. Warmth.*

"Are you okay?" Ariana looked concerned.

"I'm just fine. I'm really amazingly okay and…" *Careful…* She forced a smile. "I'm all right."

"I don't want us to be enemies, Lynnie. I really don't. I want us to stay as close as possible. We *are* sisters, you know."

Once again, she struggled to maintain an inner calm.

Ariana wants to stay close. This is getting to be a little too much for me to deal with.

The heat rushed back. She fought hard to resist it.

Please…bring back the sunshine, the warmth… The feelings of bliss…

"Don't you feel the same way, Lynnie? I know what I did the other day. I know it was wrong, too."

"Why'd you do it, then?"

Ariana focused on nudging something barely visible from her lap. "I…don't know. It…just happened. I went over to give Frank some legal papers he needed…for one of his Hedge Fund accounts—"

"And while you were there, you decided to have sex with him?"

"As I just said, it just happened. I can't explain it. And I really feel badly about it. I always will. Especially since…since—"

"Since the man's dead now?"

Ariana didn't reply.

Lynn forced herself to stay in control. *Keep the anger away. The hatred. The darkness. The hurt. Focus on trying to bring back the warmth.*

Where in heaven's name had those warm, bright feelings gone?

Will they ever come back?

Gentle. Soft. Peace. Tranquility. A bright, sunny day.

Lynn concentrated on the warm images. After about a minute, she gave her sister the most pleasant look she could manage. "I understand." It took every ounce of self-control she had. Once it felt right, the darkness drifted away, and she finally sensed the comforting brightness coming back.

"Really?" Ariana stood up. Her eyes were moist again, but she was smiling. "You actually *forgive* me?"

Lynn struggled to stay focused. "Yes, Ariana. I forgive you."

Ariana rushed over for another hug.

Later, as she followed Ariana out of the store and stood out on the sidewalk, watching as her sister marched toward the law offices just one block away, she caught something fluttering around her, quite close to her face.

A beautiful monarch butterfly flittered on her shoulder. It jumped closer and tapped her earlobe with the tip of its wing.

Just as it hopped higher up, preparing to land on her head, she noticed nearly a dozen more swooping down from the sky, heading her way.

Chapter 20

At five o'clock, while Lynn stood at the register, doing the day's tallies, the cowbell above the door clanged.

She looked up from the register. Her heart skipped a beat.

Frank's father, Ralph, was coming into the store.

Shrinking a little, Lynn felt her pulse fluttering as the man quickly invaded her space. His tense expression conveyed the unmistakable message that he was much more angry than grief-stricken regarding the news about his son. This alone told her that their encounter would not be pleasant. The warmth and brightness she'd been enjoying since Ariana had left just hours ago had quickly vanished. The memory of the butterflies dimmed as well.

Lynn had never liked Frank's father very much. The man was short-tempered and abrupt, and made no effort to hide his emotions or his strong opinions. She'd gotten along with him the few times she and Frank had visited him, but since Frank was dead, Lynn suspected that whatever pleasantness there had been before was forever gone.

Lynn could feel the counter tremble slightly as he marched right over to the register. He stopped about a foot away, his arms crossed, his broad, brooding face as foreboding as that of a Rottweiler protecting its territory. He didn't say a word and, as his cold, dark eyes fixed on her, she could feel the darkness coming back.

"Hello, Ralph," she said softly. "I'm very, very sorry about—"

"We need to talk somewhere privately." He kept his cold, unflinching gaze on her. "I don't wish to discuss anything out here in the open, with everyone in this damned store listening."

Lynn gestured toward the office door. Her nerves quivered as she led the way in. Ralph stomped past her. She closed the door and gestured for him to sit in the chair facing the desk. He hesitated, scanning the room and scowling at her collection of bird woodcarvings displayed prominently on the shelves of the bookcase covering the opposite wall. Then, after a few more tense moments, he unbuttoned his jacket and lowered his sizeable butt into the chair.

Lynn sat down facing him. Her pulse continued racing, but she told herself she could get through this. She had to, didn't she? Right now, she saw no other option. "Would you like some coffee? Jodi just made some, and it's probably still—"

"I'm good." He continued glaring.

Lynn tried relaxing, but the darkness emanating from him prevented anything warm or comforting to drift her way.

After a moment or two of uncomfortable silence, he said, "What the hell happened?"

Lynn took a breath and collected her thoughts. After all, she had nothing to hide. It wasn't as if anyone could suspect anything suspicious about all this, was there? Frank's death was an accident, and everyone knew accidents happened all the time.

"Well, Frank was crossing the street and—"

"He was hit by a van. Yeah. These cops told me the same damned thing." He sat forward. "But just to give you a heads-up, I don't believe a word of it."

"But that's exactly what—"

"You're trying to tell me my son was crossing the street when he was run down by an idiot driving a goddamned *van*? And that's *it*? The whole story?"

She forced herself to stay focused. She should have known this man would make something more out of this. Ralph Alden was as bull-headed as they came. And right now, he wanted to know what happened. The cops had already told him, but he didn't believe them. They were obviously hiding something. Or maybe they were just too stupid to figure out what really happened. It just didn't make any sense. Ralph's precious son couldn't possibly have died under such careless circumstances. Frank was just like his dad. Special. Brilliant. Perceptive. A man among men. Idiots were run down crossing the street. Slugs of society died stupidly all the time. Walking vermin unworthy of humane consideration left this earth without so much as a tear being shed for them. Morons. Drunks. Meth heads. They all died as the result of their own worthless, pitiful lifestyle.

Not brilliant, successful men like Frank Alden.

She found herself struggling to maintain an air of confidence. That was what happened, and that was what she was going to tell the man. What could

181

he do? What could he say? His son was struck by a passing van. Now he was dead. Case closed.

And no matter how difficult this was to accept, Ralph Alden could not possibly change the method in which his precious son had departed from this life.

"That's exactly what happened," she managed.

The man's scowl remained. So did the unflinching stare. After an uncomfortably long pause, he said, "They also told me he'd just come from your place shortly before he was run down. Is this true?"

She nodded.

He sat glaring at her, no doubt trying to penetrate her brain, searching for holes, lies, discrepancies—anything that would put his restless mind to rest. Anything that would make something more noble—more meaningful—about his son's death. She didn't want to say or hint at anything that might make him the least bit suspicious. Telling him anything but the honest truth could easily turn this situation extremely volatile, and she knew to choose her words wisely. This was not a man she wanted in her life. He had all sorts of connections and knew exactly how to get people to do things for him. He wasn't a nice man and was quite comfortable holding a grudge.

"Had Frank been drinking when he left your place?"

She almost sighed in relief. This was something she could be totally honest about. Everyone knew Frank Alden was a drinker—especially his father.

Frank was like his dad in many ways. His penchant for Scotch was merely one of their similarities.

"He'd had some Scotch before he left."

The man went silent again. His cold gaze never left her. Then, just when she thought he might be running out of ideas, he asked, "How much did he have?"

"How *much*?"

"Yeah. Scotch. As in, how much did he have? To drink?" The man appeared even more irritated. "What the hell else have we been talking about?"

"I honestly don't know. He—"

"You don't know how much my son had to drink while he was in your own home?"

Easy... She wanted to scold herself. That did sound stupid. It would be best to carefully weigh her words before she said anything else. Otherwise, this man would be here much longer than she wanted him to be.

"He'd been drinking before he came to visit me. I could smell it on his breath the moment he walked through the door. While he was at my place, he had about half a glass. It was one of my large glasses, maybe twelve ounces. He filled about half the glass—his usual amount. That made it about six ounces. And when he left, the glass was empty." She sensed the calmness returning and felt much more confident. "Does that answer your question?"

He thought that over.

Watching him closely, Lynn calmly waited for some other bomb to drop.

183

"Frank could handle his Scotch..." It sounded like he was talking to himself.

She said nothing.

"Was he troubled in any way? Upset? Could you tell if something was bothering him?" He stared intently at her before he spoke again. "Or did the two of you have words?"

Lynn immediately grew tense. She could feel the brightness leaving her and feared the darkness pouring freely from the man would overwhelm her. His darkness seemed to be blending with hers, causing whatever brightness still clinging to her to dim.

Taking control again, she fought to recall what he'd just asked her.

He wants to know if we had words...

Her first instinct was to refrain from telling him anything. It wasn't any of his business, for one thing, and would make this visit even more intolerable. He already blamed her for his son's death; she didn't want to give him something else he could use.

But if I don't say anything, he'll be on me like a hawk on a field mouse...

Her thoughts went right back to her exchange with the Wheeling cop and the tow truck operator. And, of course, with her recent talk with her sister.

Be careful... You can handle this, but only if you think it through and stay objective.

And above all, keep your thoughts warm and bright.

When she started talking, what came out of her mouth surprised her so much that she wondered if it had developed from her own brain. "Have you had any sleep lately, Ralph? You look really tired."

"*Huh?*"

"You obviously haven't slept in a while. When did the police call you about Frank?"

He gazed at her, perhaps trying to figure out what she was getting at. "Yesterday morning, around nine. Why do you ask? Why is this important? And what the hell does it have to do with--"

"I was just thinking that you're very tired and need your rest. This has been very difficult and extremely stressful for you. I realize you've got arrangements to make..."

He rubbed his eyes. She sensed that the darkness around him had dimmed. "I do, as a matter of fact. For one thing, I've got to get in touch with his mother. I have to find out if these damned cops called Laraine yet. They said they did, but I really need to see it through. It's a damned shame, but you just can't trust people to do their job these days."

Lynn immediately felt the tension dissolving between them. "You'd better find out for sure. It would be very cruel for her not to know what's going on."

He sat back and closed his eyes. He suddenly looked exhausted.

"It's the right thing to do." She felt the darkness inside her dimming as well. "You'll feel very good about it. So will Laraine. Frank would want the two of you to keep it together for something like this."

He opened his mouth to say something.

"Don't you think Frank would want that?"

He rubbed the back of his thick neck. Then he got up slowly and turned for the door. "Yeah. You're right. Of course he'd want that."

"That sounds like a plan to me."

Without another word, he trudged over to the door, pulled it open and slipped through the archway.

The brightness caressing her had quickly become extremely warm.

Chapter 21

Frank's mother showed up the next morning.

After visiting Lynn briefly at her shop, she left with her husband to book a room at the Holiday Inn.

As Lynn had expected, the woman's visit had not been pleasant. She was clearly devastated over the loss of her son and wasn't the least bit self-conscious about demonstrating her grief. Laraine sat in the chair facing the desk, her handkerchief covering her blotched face, her tears flowing freely. Her husband stood behind her, his hands on her shoulders while trying to console her as subtly as he possibly could. Lynn wanted to be as understanding and as sensitive as possible, but the woman was incoherent, frequently interrupting her loud sobbing with little anecdotes about something cute or interesting Frank had done as a child.

That weekend, after the Mass at the Catholic church and the short trip to the cemetery, Lynn stood off by herself as the priest spoke solemnly over the brightly polished casket. She barely heard anything going on around her. She discovered that watching the colorful wooded hills beyond the cemetery helped considerably, calming her as well as isolating her from the mourners as well as the service itself.

She needed isolation now. In fact, she craved it. She didn't even want to be here in the first place. Although she'd forgiven Frank in her heart and no longer experienced any darkness accompanying her thoughts of him, she realized that she desperately wanted to continue on with her life. So, while calming herself by focusing on the woods straight ahead, she told herself that her being here was necessary. This would be the closing of a chapter in her life that needed to be closed, and that in just a few minutes, she would be able to walk away and start her new chapter without sadness or regret.

Then, during her meditation, she caught movement out of the corner of her eye. Ariana adjusting her veil, apparently. Her sister stood just twenty feet to her left in her stylish black suit and matching hat, trying very hard to be both inconspicuous and striking while demonstrating her grieving with an occasional sob, sniff, or shudder.

Lynn went right back to watching the woods. Ariana's very presence was a grim reminder of what had happened, why they were all here in the first place. Although Lynn suspected Ariana did indeed feel considerable guilt about all this, she knew that her relationship with her sister could never be the same, and that every time she saw or thought about Ariana, the hurt and the betrayal would return, creating a significant wedge between them.

Their parents remained close, standing directly behind Lynn. They hadn't exactly warmed up to Frank during her relationship with him and hadn't said much at all about the whole thing. They'd come to the funeral strictly for moral support, keeping themselves close.

Despite a full week of endless soul-searching, Lynn still didn't know how she should feel about all this. Knowing full well that her powers of suggestion should not totally be ignored, she just could not shake her strong sense of guilt. And despite her overwhelming belief that logic and common sense should automatically dispel her fears, she knew there would always be that nagging shred of doubt plaguing her for the rest of her days.

But she also knew that, as horrible as it was, it had happened for the best. If she and Frank had eventually married, the union wouldn't have lasted. Frank clearly wasn't the same man she'd fallen in love with. In time, he would have broken her heart.

She remained standing in the same place long after the priest and most of the mourners had left. Frank's mother hugged her briefly, whispering incoherent things in her ear between sobs. Then, lowering her veil, she let her husband lead her away.

Frank's father ignored her, frowning at the casket, the priest, the woods and the funeral party. He didn't even look in her direction after everyone had turned away from the grave and slowly began the long, silent procession down the grassy hill, where the limousines were parked.

Ariana and their parents waited until everyone else had passed before moving closer. Mom and Dad hugged Lynn, patted her back gently and whispered a few kind words.

"You'll be all right, baby," her father said softly, a tired smile touching his rough features. "It was a tough break, but you're a strong girl."

"Thanks, Dad."

189

"We're here for ya. I hope you'll never forget that."

"I won't." She forced a smile.

"We liked Frank, honey," Momma said softly, sniffing. "We didn't know him very well, but he seemed quite taken by you."

"Yes, Momma."

"You'll mend." Momma gently squeezed her hands. "You're a pretty girl. You're also bright and talented. And you're still young. You have a tremendous future ahead of you. You'll find someone else."

She nodded dutifully, forced another quick smile, and sighed as they gave her one last nod, turned and went down the hill.

Ariana hugged her briefly, pulled away, forced a teary smile, sniffed, and sighed heavily. Then she turned around and rejoined their parents.

Lynn stood before the grave a few more minutes and wondered once again how she should feel about all this. Should she be experiencing remorse? A sense of loss? Should she be sobbing? Crying? Struggling with the impulse of tearing her hair out?

Shouldn't she feel that her world had just collapsed right out from under her?

After all, the man she'd known intimately for several years was dead. He was gone forever.

Not one tear nudged its way down her cheek. And aside from a few sleepless nights, she didn't once entertain the desire to head off to the local pharmacy in search of meds.

Shouldn't she be devastated by all this?

Shouldn't she be the least bit penitent? Especially since she was so certain that the man was dead because of her? Of something she thought? Or wished?

A butterfly flitted over, settling on her shoulder. Moments later, another skimmed past, turning in midflight and landing on her veil. It seemed to be looking at her, and for a moment she wondered if it was actually one of the spirit lady's butterflies that had flown all the way from her abandoned home to see how she was doing. She smiled at it and was ready to say something when it took off. Two more flew over, settling on her forearms. Another one. Then another.

The warmth caressed her softly.

Despite the sudden relief, she went back to gazing at the grave.

You did this yourself, Frank... She took in a breath of fresh air while trying desperately not to glare at the casket. *You cheated on me with my own sister, and now you're dead, and although I've forgiven you, I just can't find it in my heart to think of you with any fondness. I'm not glad you're dead, but I am glad that I didn't marry you. I don't know where your spirit is right now, but I do know that it isn't with me. But if it was, I'd like to think that I'd also feel your shame, as well as your guilt. This way, I could forgive your spirit just as I've forgiven your betrayal.*

These thoughts finally out of her system, she turned away.

As she started down the hill where her Honda was parked, she noticed that the butterflies had disappeared.

She was all alone again.

And despite all her efforts to keep her thoughts bright and cheerful, some of the dreaded darkness and cold had trickled back.

Chapter 22

The following Monday morning, just moments after Jodi had unlocked the front door of the shop, the cowbell clanged loudly, and the door swished open.

Ralph Alden bullied his way into the store. Looking just as arrogant and determined as he'd been during his first visit, he marched right over to where Lynn had just started rearranging one of the window displays. He stood over her, his hands on his hips as his dark, unflinching gaze settled on her.

Sighing tiredly, she straightened and returned his gaze. During the last few days she'd learned that, above all else, she should keep calm. She'd also learned that whatever had happened in the Enlightenment Room had done much to dictate what happened in whatever situation she faced in the future. As she regarded the tense, troubled man facing her, she sensed anxiety, confusion, and rage. She strongly suspected that Ralph Alden was about to demand more answers to his son's sudden death.

"Hello, Ralph." A strange sense of peace settled over her, and she quickly found that she wasn't the least bit frightened or intimidated. "What brings you here? I thought you would have gone back long before—"

"We need to talk."

"About what?"

His deep-set eyes remained glaring. "I'm pretty sure you know the answer to that."

It was necessary to downplay this. Otherwise, the man would smell fear, which would once again arouse his suspicions. "I really don't, but whatever it is, it seems important."

"It is. In fact, it's *very* important."

She shrugged. "Would you like to talk in my office?"

"I can't think of anything I'd like better."

She turned. "Jodi? Would you mind handling things for a few minutes?"

Jodi looked up from the register and gave Ralph a brief smile. "Not at all."

Lynn led the way into her office.

The instant she closed the door, Ralph took a deep breath and began glaring at the floor. She knew something bad was coming but decided that whatever it was, she could handle it. The mysterious calm settling within her remained strong. "Something on your mind?" she asked.

"Did you honestly think you could keep the details of my son's death from me?"

"I beg your pardon?"

"Don't try and play innocent with me, young lady. I've been around the block quite a few times."

The heat radiating from the man had increased considerably. Lynn slipped past him and sat down at her desk. Instinct told her that the best way of handling this was to let him have his say. She was quite confident that his ranting wouldn't bother her. She'd just send him on his way when he'd finished, then continue her daily activities in the store. "I honestly don't know what you're talking about."

He came closer and stood over her desk, as a hungry lion would tower over its next meal. "Then maybe I need to put this another way. Something that might just shed a tad more light on this matter. For both of us." He paused before he spoke again. "To make a long story short, I just had a lengthy discussion with your sister."

Lynn had no problem returning the man's cold stare with one of casual indifference. She'd discovered that despite her initial reaction, that strange calm that had settled within her had not budged. This man had talked to Ariana. And Ariana, always a coward under pressure, probably told him exactly what happened between her and Frank.

So, what did this mean, exactly? Would it explain anything more about Frank's death? Would it tell Ralph what he really wanted to know? Put his fears and suspicions to rest? Give him closure? End the mystery, once and for all?

It most likely wouldn't do any of those things. Ralph Alden just wouldn't accept his son's sudden death and was searching for anything that would shed a different light on things. In the man's arrogant, twisted mind, Frank simply shouldn't be dead. He was Ralph's sole heir. But now that he was dead, things would have to be rewritten, while other things would have to be reworked. And because of all this, someone should have to pay dearly.

And since Ralph couldn't accept what had happened and wanted someone to atone for whatever *did* happen, he planned to stay in town and play the amateur detective until he'd exhausted all efforts to get the facts down—at least for his own personal satisfaction.

But no matter how hard he tried, Lynn wasn't about to play into his scheme. Not very long ago, this man would have succeeded in his personal little game of manipulation and terror. He would have intimidated and terrified her, eventually bullying her into telling him every single detail of whatever he wanted to know. But after what had happened in Bridgeport, Lynn discovered that she had somehow grown considerably stronger. She didn't know if it was because of what had happened in the Enlightenment Room or because she'd managed to escape the Pozner brothers using her intelligence and gut instinct. She only knew that Ralph Alden could no longer frighten her.

"Care to add anything to that?" Ralph finally asked.

"To what?"

He groaned. "To anything your sister might have said…"

"I don't know if I can."

"And why the hell is that?"

"To make it simple, I have absolutely no idea what Ariana said to you. So how could I possibly add to that?"

He stared at her, trembling a little. She could tell what he was thinking. He'd planned a mental battle. What he didn't know was that he had no chance of winning.

"You know what she said, so let's stop the bullshit right now and get right down to it."

She sat back in her chair. "As I just said, I have no idea what my sister told you."

It took him a few moments to accept the fact that she was going to hold her ground. "All right, then. Since you apparently don't wish to cooperate... Your sister and my son...well, to put it bluntly, let's just say they did the dirty deed and you found out about it firsthand."

It was easy to visualize what happened. Ralph Alden glaring, getting close, putting his hands on his hips to make himself larger and even more intimidating. Ariana cowering as usual during a confrontation, struggling to hide inside herself.

"Ariana told you that?" she asked.

"You're damned right she did."

"She just came right out...and confessed?"

"Not right off, but after I insisted, she came to her senses."

"You *insisted*?"

"I'd say I was forced to."

"You bullied her."

"I wouldn't call it bullying, per se... Not exactly. I just insisted—as I said."

Lynn knew full well what happened. This loud, arrogant bastard had scared her sister half to death.

"Care to substantiate what she told me?"

Lynn returned the man's cold gaze, knowing full well that if he thought this would go easy, he was in for a rude awakening. "I'd like you to tell me something first."

197

"And what would that be?"

"Just what exactly does my sister's indiscretions have to do with Frank crossing the street and being struck down by a passing van?"

Ralph sat forward in his chair. His dark glare did not waver. "You're changing the damned subject."

"I'm only interested in where you're going with what you've just told me."

"Let's make it simple, then. I want you to tell me exactly what happened. Why my son left your apartment when he did and was killed by a passing van the moment he crossed the street."

This man was desperately searching for something he could use to explain all this. Something he could blame her for. But she knew better. There was no way she could suffer any degree of prosecution for the accident. Even though she suspected she might have been the reason Frank was dead, there was no way it could be proven. Frank had cheated on her. Now he was dead. And nothing could change that.

"You're absolutely right," she said. "You're entitled to the truth. So here it is. Your son had sex with my kid sister. I found out about it when I went over to his house and caught them in the act. Frank came to see me Saturday night. He'd been drinking and wanted to apologize for his behavior. He asked if he could have a drink. I told him to help himself. He tried apologizing and I told him I didn't want to see him again. Then I told him to leave, and he left. This happened probably no more than a minute or

198

so before he was struck down by the van." She sat back. "Is that all you wanted to know?"

He continued glaring at her. After what seemed a very long time, he rose slowly from his chair and looked down at her. She could feel the anger emanating from him in blistering waves. "*You* caused his death."

"Actually, the van caused his death."

"You cold bitch. You're sitting there, telling me that my son tried apologizing to you for an indiscretion, and you responded by telling him to leave your apartment."

"That's exactly what I did. And that's exactly what happened."

"You're showing absolutely no remorse for any of this."

"You're absolutely right."

"You didn't even show any grief at the funeral."

"Right again."

"How can you be so cold? My son loved you. He would have probably asked you to marry him. What I've learned from all this—what you've just told me by your attitude, and by your vicious choice of words—is that he never really knew your true nature."

"There's nothing wrong with my true nature. Most of the people who know me would say I'm a very warm person."

"Then how can you sit there and not show any sort of remorse for my son's—"

"Your son hurt me very deeply. In fact, he hurt me so much that I was much too angry with him to grieve for him. He shouldn't have done what he did. There was no reason for it. My sister, of all people? Even a man like you should be able to understand why I couldn't let something like that slide."

"And *this* is why you tossed him out of your apartment?"

"It's why I told him to leave, yes."

"Don't you realize that, by tossing him out, you sent him into a severe state of depression that blew away his logical mental processes, which ultimately caused him to cross the street at the wrong time?"

"That's probably exactly why it happened that way."

He remained standing there, still trembling, his fierce dark eyes boring into her.

Lynn could feel the darkness returning. This time, she made no effort to keep it away. She wanted this man out of her office and out of her life. She didn't want to see him again. And she didn't expect to see sunshine or experience heavenly warmth while feeling this way.

After the heated moment passed, he said, "This is insane. This is totally intolerable." He took a breath, and what sounded like a labored groan escaped his throat. "I'm going to report this matter to the authorities, and then we'll see what can be done about some sort of wrongful death civil suit—"

"Actually, you're not going to do that."

"W-What?"

"What you're going to do is leave my office. Then you're going to get in your car and drive away, and you're not going to give this matter another thought—"

"How *dare* you threaten me—"

"I'm not threatening you at all. I'm telling you this because I don't want anything to happen to you."

He looked like a man about to have a heart attack. "I can't...I just can't believe the vicious way you're talking to me. You obnoxious bitch—"

"As I just said, I'm not threatening you. I'm telling you to do exactly as I've said because it's in your best interest to do so."

"I can't believe this. You're a horrible woman. I can't understand what my son saw in you. I'm gonna go through with a civil suit, and I believe I'm about to add a few choice items to it. My attorneys shouldn't have much of a problem with—"

"If I were you, I'd leave this office right now."

Just then, the darkness slammed through her. She rubbed her temples and took a deep breath. Moments later, the darkness dimmed. She sat back and waited anxiously for the warmth to return. It didn't come back immediately, but after a few tense moments, she began feeling a little better.

Still trembling, Ralph Alden remained staring at her. He wanted to say something, but his jaw was trembling so much, he couldn't get the words out. He looked like he was about to collapse.

Please don't, she thought wildly, her pulse racing. *Please don't drop dead in my office. Please do as I've said. Please go back to your home in Ligonier.*

After about a minute, his darkness dimmed, and he seemed to be calming down. With a deep sigh, he turned toward the doorway and stormed out of the office.

Lynn remained in her chair, trying to calm herself. Once the darkness subsided, she got up and left the room.

There was no sign of him in the store. No sign of him out in the street.

She went back to her office, sat back down, and closed her eyes. For the next fifteen minutes, she sat in silence, the darkness around her gradually vanishing.

When she felt the brightness drifting back, she got back up and left the store.

Outside, the sun was shining.

She stood there beneath the green awning, waiting for the warmth to come back.

After about fifteen minutes, a large black, yellow-spotted butterfly swooped down from the awning. It hopped over to the park bench and stood there for a few moments, watching her. Then it jumped up and flew away.

Chapter 23

The next morning, Lynn, dressed in her maroon bathrobe and fuzzy white slippers, went out to her tiny backyard carrying a cup of freshly brewed coffee. Taking in the sweetness of the morning air, she lowered herself into her lounge chair.

It was a bright, sunny morning. She could hear the birds chirping from the trees. In this cheerful setting, she sincerely hoped it would be a beautiful day filled with positive sensations and the promise of happy times to follow. If her feelings of hope rang true, Ralph Alden would have already left St. Clairsville and driven back home. And if things chose to happen the way they should, the man would never return to infect her life with hatred, anger, darkness and despair.

She leaned her head back and focused on coaxing the warm sensations to return. To rid her spirit of every trace of darkness still clinging to her. To embrace every positive image she could conjure up in her mind.

A yellow butterfly appeared, leaping over the privacy fence separating her yard from her neighbor's. It flitted over to one of the flowers in her tiny garden. After briefly sipping its nectar, it darted away and disappeared behind the fence.

After that, there was nothing. The birds continued chirping, but there were no more butterflies.

She waited a few more minutes.

Nothing changed.

A couple of minutes later, the birds stopped chirping. All she heard from then on were traffic sounds rushing up and down on Main.

She remained sitting there, alone and isolated, struggling to keep from growing depressed. There were no more bird sounds, indicating that they must have flown away.

A sick, empty feeling developed in her gut. Why was this happening? The darkness had dimmed, but the warmth had not returned. No warmth, no brightness. And for some reason, the warm sensation of happiness she wanted so much to return just hadn't come back.

This wasn't right. She hadn't wished any ill will upon Ralph Alden. None whatsoever. She'd merely wanted him out of her office. She'd also wanted him to go back to his home, where he could continue living his life again. She'd even told him that she didn't want anything to happen to him.

But in spite of all that, the brightness hadn't returned.

She waited ten more minutes. The traffic sounds persisted, drowning out everything else.

Why couldn't she bring back the brightness and the warmth?

Where in heaven's name had all the good stuff gone?

***

The workday crept by very slowly.

Customers came in, browsed, smiled politely, and left. Several asked a question or two while most

204

of the others dropped by the bins advertising the daily specials, rummaged through, found a poster or a print they liked, or just shrugged, waved, and left.

Lynn remained in the background. Still gun-shy over Frank's death and her unpleasant encounter with his father, she let Jodi do the heavy lifting with customer interactions while confining herself to less stressful activities, such as greeting, pointing, smiling, and answering simple questions.

Just before lunch, as she did the morning tallies at the computer in her office, she thought about her future and wondered how she was going to deal with customers, managers, buyers—people, period—since her strange experience in the Enlightenment Room. She tried convincing herself that her encounter with Ralph was a one-time thing, and since she'd been on her guard, he'd left safely, and without any hint of catastrophe following him.

She decided that her meeting with Ralph was one of an extreme nature and would never be repeated. Her encounter with Laraine hadn't ended in tragedy, did it? Neither did her visit with Ariana. Or with the Wheeling cop and the tow truck driver.

So why should she be paranoid at all?

The whole idea was silly to begin with. Just because Frank had died in a freak accident didn't mean that every battle she would have with anyone from now on would cause something awful to happen. She'd always been proud of her people skills—why should she think that a sudden enhancement of her moods would endanger everyone she ever faced for the rest of her life?

That afternoon, as she closed the register and tried focusing on lunch, Jodi came back from her morning deposit at the bank. Her face was as white as a sheet, her eyes moist and blood-shot. She was trembling.

Lynn followed her into the office and closed the door. Although the store was empty, Lynn sensed her friend's distress and feared that whatever had happened needed to be discussed in private. "What's wrong? You look like…like you've just seen a—"

"Something terrible has happened." Jody brought her fists up to her mouth. Her mascara had smeared her cheeks. She wanted to speak, but her lips quivered too much.

"Jodi, *please* tell me what's—"

Jodi took a breath and tried collecting herself. "It's…it's Mr. Alden."

The back of Lynn's neck turned cold. It was as if someone had just pressed a cold washrag to her skin. "What about him?"

Jodi swallowed audibly. After three more tries, she was finally able to get the words out. "He's…he's *dead*…"

Lynn's heart crawled slowly up her throat. She tried forcing it down, but it stayed right there. "What...*happened*?" The words came out sluggishly.

"I just spoke with Mr. Covington. At the bank." Jodi wiped her cheek and took a deep breath. "He said his son-in-law, the trooper with the Highway Patrol? There was a nasty accident. On the

Interstate. It happened earlier this morning. Mr. Alden... They said he lost control...of his BMW...and ran head-on...into one of those logging trucks..."

***

Lynn spent the rest of the afternoon alone in the office, struggling to understand why Frank's father had died only hours after talking to her.

It made no sense. Ralph Alden was not a careless man. In fact, he was just the opposite. Cold, calculating, and methodical. A man who'd prided himself in his decisions and his accomplishments and took great pleasure in telling anyone within earshot just how few mistakes he'd made in his life. Ralph Alden was insensitive, callous, and bull-headed.

There was nothing haphazard about him. Nothing foolhardy. After all, he'd been a CPA the last thirty years, and his life was just as orderly and as organized as his profession. Though he was grieving over the loss of his son, his granite-like constitution had made him both angry and vengeful. Even so, he certainly would not have engaged in anything that would endanger his own life.

She tried hard to rationalize his last visit and struggled to recall every last detail. Ralph had been extremely upset. Enraged. In total denial. Defiant, and more than eager to wage mortal battle with anyone who disagreed with him. His son was his pride and joy. His sole heir. The boy's death had come forty years too soon, and for no good reason. Frank had entirely too much to live for. He was

207

successful, popular, intelligent, and as healthy and fit as anyone else pushing forty.

Someone should be liable for his accidental death. Someone needed to answer for it. It was that simple. And since he couldn't go after the idiot who'd run Frank down simply because the cops had legally absolved him of the accident, Lynn was the one who should answer for it. And because Lynn hadn't shown any remorse or expressed any grief, Ralph considered her suspect. Her tone wasn't penitent enough. She hadn't even caved in when he'd threatened her with legal action. All of this proved more than enough incentive for him to begin his crusade.

But would any of this explain what had happened to him on the Interstate?

She tried once again to recall what she'd told the man after he'd threatened her with legal retaliation. However, her mind quickly turned blank and the darkness trickled back, consuming her. She'd told him to leave her office. To get in his car and drive back home.

Nothing else.

And now the man was dead.

But why had this happened? When Ralph had left her office, he'd done just as she'd suggested. It was as if he'd been in some sort of trance.

So why had he died?

Had it been the result of their last meeting?

Or was this something else entirely?

Did it have anything to do with the strange powers she'd acquired in the spirit lady's house?

208

Did it have anything to do with Lynn's dark mood? The fact that she was uncomfortable?

Or had it something to do with Ralph's darkness drifting over to intermingle with her own?

These last few random thoughts frightened her more than anything else.

Did this mean that whenever someone disagreed with her or threatened her, something terrible would happen?

A horrifying accident? Then, eventually, death?

The panic returning once again, Lynn lowered her face in her hands and began sobbing.

Through her tears, she tried desperately to figure out what could be done about this.

Once thing was certain: she couldn't continue living like this. She had to make some sort of major decision.

She wasn't prepared to spend the rest of her life causing torment and death to others.

***

To keep her mind occupied, Lynn spent the rest of the workday going through the shop's records and reworking the totals for the morning and afternoon.

However, after two hours of poring over endless columns of figures on the computer screen, her eyes glazed over and she could no longer concentrate. She found that she was hopelessly obsessed with trying to determine what had to be done to make things right again. She was reasonably certain she'd caused two terrible deaths and feared that if she didn't find some way of dealing with this, others might die as well.

To give herself a break, she went back out into the store and spent time tending to the few late-afternoon customers while Jodi handled things at the register.

At around four, Jodi left the store to get two slices of strawberry cheesecake from the bakery across the street.

As they sat in the office, enjoying their cheesecake and a batch of freshly brewed vanilla coffee, Lynn stared at the hazy beams of afternoon sun drifting in through the open blinds and wondered if she'd ever see the butterflies again. Or if she'd ever be happy again. Or carefree.

Or, more important than anything else, if she'd ever become her old self.

She began thinking of Margaret Freedman and wondered if she'd ever see her again. Then she wondered what she'd say to the spirit lady if they ever did meet again.

The moment that thought entered her mind, her anger flared right up. She realized right then that she blamed the spirit lady for everything that had been happening lately and hoped she could be given the opportunity to tell her how her visit to the Enlightenment Room had completely ruined her life.

"I found out something about Ralph Alden." Jodi looked troubled as she sat beside the desk, carefully slicing a sliver of cheesecake with her fork.

Lynn snapped out of her daze as if she were just slapped. "What's that?"

"Something about Ralph Alden I just learned."

Lynn was afraid to ask. "What about him?"

"He wasn't drunk."

"Are you sure?"

"Uh-huh…"

Lynn shrunk in her seat. This meant something else had happened. Something strange. Something she didn't really want to know.

"I mean, are you really and truly certain?"

Jodi nodded grimly.

Lynn found that she couldn't speak, couldn't even move. This was something she had hoped would clear up the mystery. Something that could shed some light on what had happened. And something that would help her feel less guilty.

Jodi had a sip of coffee. "Mr. Covington was at the bakery when I went over for the cheesecake. He said his son-in-law had called him a little earlier. The medical examiner checked Ralph's blood, said the blood alcohol level registered less than point oh-eight. If he'd been drinking, it wasn't much. Even if he *had* been drinking, it had been more than an hour, maybe even two or three hours, since his last drink and before he got in his car."

Lynn didn't reply. This was awful news. Now she knew for sure that the man's sudden demise had nothing to do with alcohol.

It was because of me. The very thought made her want to pull her hair out. *It was me and what I'd said to him. I caused his death. I was the one who killed the man—just as I'd killed Frank.*

"Lynn? Did you hear me?"

Lynn nodded.

"Strange, isn't it?"

Lynn didn't reply.

"Don'tcha think?"

"Very."

"A man like him? Losing control? He was only sixty-four, you know."

"I...didn't know."

"That's not so old nowadays."

"No. It isn't."

"Makes you think—ya know?"

Lynn stared at the large wedge of uneaten cheesecake on her plate and realized she was no longer hungry. She had other things on her mind. Things much more important than a portion of uneaten cheesecake. "Yes," she said softly, still staring at her plate. "It does indeed make you think."

Chapter 24

Several days later, after many sleepless nights, Lynn reached a very difficult decision.

She had to return to Margaret Freedman's house.

It had all begun there, in the Enlightenment Room. The moods. The brightness. The darkness.

Most of all, the *power*.

It was a term she'd never wanted to use. A word she'd wanted desperately to avoid since her bizarre nightmare just a few short weeks ago. But now she realized that there was no other term that would fit.

Power. That's exactly what it was. She could easily sugarcoat it, blaming it on fate. The stars. The natural order of things. A subconscious urge. Chance. Predestination. Coincidence. Kismet.

But what it all boiled down to was the terrifying fact that ever since she'd left Margaret Freedman's house, she was able to influence people—to manipulate them—into doing exactly what she wanted them to do.

A Wheeling cop and a tow truck operator had both walked away—without towing her car or giving her a ticket—just minutes after she'd given them the suggestion.

Frank and his father were both dead because of the dark emotions she'd experienced emanating from them. Because their feelings had meshed with hers.

Everything that had happened to her from the time Bryan Grant had taken her back to Wheeling had been the direct result of the short time she'd spent in Margaret Freedman's Enlightenment Room.

Was it indeed kismet? Was it karma?

Was it some bizarre form of mind control the spirit lady had given her as a token of her gratitude for their new friendship?

Or was it witchcraft?

Like it or not, she had to consider it, hadn't she? Margaret Freedman was a witch, was she not? As she firmly maintained, she was a white witch. White witches were benevolent. And kind. And loving. As a white witch, the woman performed only good acts. She helped people, cast benevolent spells on them, healed them. Made them happy and fulfilled their deepest desires. She was a beautiful lady. Bright and warm.

Summed up in just a few words, Margaret Freedman was goodness in both body and spirit.

But it didn't matter, did it? Good or bad, a witch was a witch. A witch had powers. It didn't matter how she used these powers; the important thing was that she had them.

And now Lynn had them. But for some reason she just could not comprehend, her powers weren't good. They were very bad. And so were the results. A person did as she said. Otherwise, the person died. And nothing could be simpler—or more frightening—than that.

But the fact remained. Lynn hadn't been herself since she'd left Margaret Freedman's house. She knew that unless she managed to undo what had been done, her future was doomed. As long as she dealt with people, she'd have to consciously force herself from thinking certain thoughts. She'd have to somehow force the darkness away and concentrate on the light, the warmth. Wonderful thoughts. Happy thoughts. And no matter what was said or done, she'd be forced to struggle very hard to keep the darkness from smothering her. As long as the power stayed with her, people would die.

What's wrong with me? The situation suddenly seemed just as complicated as it was ridiculous. *Why can't I be content with all this? Why can't I just say hell with it and do what has suddenly come natural to me? Why can't I let nature take its course? I should just take what's mine and make those who don't agree with me suffer the ultimate sacrifice.*

Why can't I do this?

The answer was simple and came very quickly.

She just wasn't made that way. She'd never enjoyed watching people suffer and found it was infinitely worse when she realized that she was the one causing the suffering. She also never liked doing things the easy way, or taking what wasn't rightfully hers. There was just too much misery in the world already. Too much stealing. Too much hatred. And anger. And violent death. Too much of everything wrong and hurtful. Doing anything that

215

added to any of this should be considered both criminal and evil.

This was something she could never live with.

***

At 6:30, Lynn closed and locked up the shop.

While she and Jodi went out back to get into their vehicles, Lynn couldn't help wondering if she was doing the right thing. Each time she thought of what she was about to do, she realized she might be doing something very stupid and foolish. Her plan might be a very bad one. And even though her intentions were good, the very idea of confronting the spirit lady once again was, at best, something that might not end well at all.

"Are you okay?" Jodi asked as she opened the door of her Camaro.

"Why do you ask?"

Jodi shrugged. "You've been very quiet and distant for the last several days. Even now you seem very...distracted."

That was a very appropriate word. In fact, she couldn't think of a more fitting term that would describe her mood.

"I'm fine."

"See you tomorrow, then?"

Lynn waved, slid behind the wheel of her Honda, left St. Clairsville, got on the Interstate and drove directly to Bridgeport.

Traffic was heavy as usual, but she wasn't paying attention. The moment she'd pulled out onto Main Street, she began thinking about the spirit lady's house. And what she should do when she got

216

there. And what would happen if the spirit lady wasn't there when she arrived.

And, more importantly, what she should do if the spirit lady actually *was* there...

Don't think about that right now.

If she obsessed about this any further, she was afraid she'd turn off at the first exit and drive back to St. Clairsville.

It was important to think about what had happened to her in the few short weeks since she'd left the spirit lady's house. And how she felt about all of it. And how she wanted things to be. She hoped that once she stopped worrying about what she wanted to say, everything might just slip right into place.

She reached Bridgeport just twenty minutes later. After she'd stopped at the first major intersection, she experienced a brief episode of anxiety and once again considered turning around and driving back home. After all, what could she possibly accomplish, even if she did see the spirit lady again?

The harsh memories drifted right back. Before she realized it, she'd already gone through the light at the intersection and began heading south on Marion.

It was getting dark, and for one brief moment, she experienced a brain blip and suddenly realized she hadn't the foggiest notion of where she was going. But as she approached the intersection of Marion and Howard, some inner sense suggested that she turn right. In the next instant, the terrifying memories of her trip in the Pozners' battered pickup returned, and a feeling of cold numbness had soon overpowered her.

Stay focused. Don't let anything distract you.

She struggled to keep going straight and wondered what would happen if she saw those two again.

Would they remember her? Would they try doing what they'd originally intended?

I can't let this influence me.

She kept the Honda moving straight down the deteriorating road and forced herself to concentrate on her plan. If she came across them again, she was confident that she'd be able to do what needed to be done.

And what would that be? asked the strange voice in her mind. *What'll you do if they come after you again?*

Will you suggest that they get back in their pickup, drive directly to the Interstate and slam into the first logging rig they come across?

Or will you tell them to drive to one of the bars in town, order a bottle of cheap whiskey and then start a fight with the first motorcycle gang that comes into the place?

She couldn't possibly do anything like that. What she'd done with Frank had been out of anger. What happened with Ralph had been what she could only consider an unfortunate accident. She had no desire whatsoever to influence two idiots to kill themselves. The world wouldn't waste an instant mourning for them, but that wasn't why she chose

218

not to do it. It just wasn't the right thing to do. More importantly, she knew full well that she could not deliberately say or do anything that would hurt or kill anyone.

Her future, as she saw it, rested on her returning to Margaret Freedman's house. And then, of course, another visit to the Enlightenment Room. Then, finally, trying to revert back to how her life had been before.

But no matter how hard she thought about all this, she just couldn't imagine what would happen when she faced the spirit lady again.

For one thing, she didn't think she'd ever see her again. As far as she knew, when she'd come out of the Enlightenment Room, Margaret Freedman's spirit had left forever. She didn't know if it was because the spirit lady had passed over once Lynn had absorbed the powers in the room, or just decided that since another spirit had taken over, she could finally rest in peace.

Whatever the reason, Lynn feared that she didn't have many options left. She could either go on as she'd been doing—manipulating people, sending them to their individual fate—or try and reclaim her spirit as it once was.

Ten minutes later, she approached the desolate area where the road forked. Her pulse hammering, she veered left. Here, the crumbling, winding road would take her to the eerie section of the county, where the houses grew scarce and nearly invisible, and the hills extended as far as the eye could see.

Her hands had grown numb as they gripped the wheel, but she managed to keep the Honda moving. The familiar patch of road showed a dull shade of gray in her headlights. She could tell she was getting closer. It wouldn't be long at all before she'd stumble upon the deadfall that would lead her to the dirt path.

The very same path that went to the house where the white witch calling herself Margaret Freedman had once—and still— lived.

Chapter 25

Lynn coaxed the Honda to the end of the road, where the giant deadfall sprawled in the tall weeds just a few yards beyond the rusted barbed wire fence.

The shadows in her headlight beams instantly transformed the deadfall, the weed-covered hill beyond it and the surrounding trees into a collage of eerie shadows and dark figures moving about in the darkness. She sat totally still, her fists fastened to the wheel in a death-grip. Even though she clearly knew why she'd come here, she suddenly had no intention of getting out of the car. The strange shadows jumping about in her headlight beams had jinxed her, keeping her from moving.

After several minutes, her brain finally began working again, and she realized she was being silly. The headlights were creating the shadows, the breeze making the weeds and the loose limbs and twigs move around, forming skeletal figures. Nothing else, supernatural or otherwise, was going on out there.

After considerable effort, she peeled her left hand from the wheel and pressed the button to slide the window down a few inches. The cool air drifted in, relaxing her, and she discovered that she could actually listen to the gentle sounds of the night without distraction. She closed her eyes while the wind whispered softly through the trees. The distant hooting of an owl penetrated the silence. Far off in the night, the barking of dogs created a symphony of discordant sound.

No approaching footsteps.

No clicking of a gun.

No heavy breathing.

Yes, she was being silly. Did she honestly think she'd been yanked from reality and dropped into a scene from some mindless slash & gore flick? Stupid, giggling teens out for a quick romp in the woods? Heavy drinking? Everyone sharing a joint or two? Reckless groping and sex? A slobbering escapee from Moundsville lumbering after them, a blood-soaked machete in his hands?

There was nothing here to encourage her imagination to go crazy. She was out in the boonies, and yes, there were all sorts of stories and local folklore associated with this area. The Pozner boys had even boasted about such things. At the time, she thought they were just trying to scare her.

But even if any of the stories rang true, what did she have to fear?

She'd been through this before. She was kidnapped by the Pozners and brought out here. The bottom line was that she'd managed to get away from them.

And, most importantly, she'd survived.

Now she was alone, safe in her own car, but just as frightened as she'd been the first time.

What was different now?

It's me. I'm different.

This startling realization slammed into her yet again. She was indeed a changed person and feared

222

that what happened from now on would probably change her destiny for the rest of her life. The change had happened just a few short weeks ago, only a couple of yards straight ahead, just beyond the deadfall. And the hill. And the road beyond. And the steep, weed-smothered hill beyond the path.

The same path where the witch calling herself Margaret Freedman lived.

The spirit lady had said she was a good witch—one who did wonderful things for all sorts of people in the area. She was beautiful, with long, flowing red hair and dazzling blue eyes. She had a stunning smile and a soft, sensuous warmth emanating about her. A lovely woman who walked in beauty, serenaded by birds and butterflies.

A woman whose warmth radiated brightly, whose beautiful blue eyes sparkled and whose hair glittered in the sunlight.

A woman who appeared to Lynn from beyond the grave because their auras had somehow connected.

A woman who said she and Lynn were kindred spirits.

A woman who had done something to Lynn that turned her spirit dark and cold.

A woman who had turned her into a murderer.

***

Lynn got out of the Honda.

Her penlight pointed straight ahead, she focused the slender beam of white light directly on the deadfall.

223

The anger, the disgust, and the humiliation of what had happened to her had repressed her fears, urging her forward.

Kindred spirits. Connecting auras.

She paraded me into her den of darkness and spoke nonsense to me. And all the while, every single particle of negative energy in that room penetrated my spirit.

She suspected that all the dark elements lingering in that room all these many years had bombarded her, changing her essence into something dark, something cold.

Something unrecognizable.

Something evil.

She turned me into a disgustingly evil creature causing death and destruction.

The only thing registering in her brain in that one bleak, unrelenting moment was that she had to do whatever it took to get her former spirit back.

And with these images flowing heavily in her mind, she approached the barbed wire fence. Then, using her penlight to locate a gap large enough, she slipped through and approached the deadfall.

***

Guided by the tiny beam of her penlight, she elbowed her way through the jagged branches, vines and brush, stepping over the long, twisted rows of dead limbs blocking the path leading to the weed-covered hill.

Just beyond it, the line of trees would lead her directly to the winding road covered in pine needles.

Keeping the light beam pointed straight ahead, she spotted the huge shadows of the familiar path that would take her to the hill leading to Margaret Freedman's old house.

Her skin tingled as the memories cascaded wildly in her head. Images of that fateful night flew past and she found that she needed to stop for a few moments to close her eyes and concentrate on getting her nerves under control.

Once again, the cold, dark thoughts made her decision for her.

She was nice to me. Warm and friendly. She told me we were kindred spirits...

And then she let the darkness in her special room turn me into some evil thing.

The anger climbed hotly up her back, and before she knew it, she realized that she'd resumed walking. About twenty yards farther down, she paused where the break in the tree line led to the steep hill that swept up to the house at its crest.

You can do this. You've done it before. You can do it again.

Taking a deep breath, she pointed the light beam at the break and resumed moving forward.

Just as she was about to slip past the trees, a soft, high-pitched voice behind her said, "A witch lives up there, on top of the hill."

Startled, she froze. The voice was that of a child. She feared that after she'd turned around, she'd be facing a little boy and his little gray dog. And after she'd finished talking to them, the boy and his dog would turn away, cross the road and disappear amongst the trees and the tall weeds.

She tried to recall what Bryan Grant had said about them. Then she remembered that Bryan didn't live here and knew virtually nothing about any of the locals.

But what really puzzled her wasn't the identity of the boy, but why he was out walking his dog in the middle of the woods at this time of night. Judging by the darkness, she suspected that it was probably at least an hour—maybe even two hours—since she'd left the store. This made it around 8:30 or 9:00. Not terribly late, but out here, in the middle of nowhere, she suspected that the boy's parents were already worrying about his whereabouts.

She turned and pointed the light. Sure enough, it was the same boy she'd talked to before. The dog was also the same cute little critter wagging its tail, just as it had the first time she'd encountered them.

"Do you remember talking to me before?" she asked uneasily.

The boy shrugged. "I can't see your face. Too dark."

Lynn brought up the penlight and pointed the slender beam at her face.

The moment the light illuminated her features, the boy's jaw dropped. Gasping, he backed up. The dog yipped and circled around until he was behind the boy. The boy trembled. His eyes filled the sockets. His voice sounded choked as he whispered, "You're her!"

Lynn could not speak.

The boy backed up another step or two. The dog whined softly.

Lynn cleared her throat. She was about to ask the boy what he meant when the two little figures spun around, darted across the road and disappeared in the weeds.

Vanished. Without a trace. Or a sound.

She pointed her beam in the direction the two had gone. The weeds swayed in the cool evening breeze. Otherwise, she saw no sign of a disturbance.

And no sign of the boy or his little dog.

Lynn swallowed a lump in her throat.

What on earth was all that about?

Were the boy and his dog there in the first place?

Of course they were. She'd seen them. Talked to them. Heard the boy speak, the dog yip. They were both there. Just a few feet away. They were real. But now they were gone.

You weren't imagining them. They were right there. Just a couple of feet from where you're now standing.

Then it dawned on her what the boy had said.

"You're her!"

Reality sliced into her. Chills ran down her spine, and she shivered in the cool night air.

My God... He thought I was the witch. He saw me in the light and was totally convinced I'm the witch living in the house at the top of the hill.

The spirit lady really and truly has turned me into a witch!

227

Fueled by a fresh surge of heat, Lynn slipped through the break in the tree line and began scaling the steep, brush-covered hill.

Chapter 26

Large packing boxes covered the front porch of Margaret Freedman's house.

There were four rows of them., stacked three high, making each pile nearly six feet tall. Some sort of sign or poster on a wire base leaned against the front wall next to the door.

Lynn squeezed between the stacks and aimed her beam of light at it. And gasped.

It was a *FOR SALE* sign. A white strip announcing *SOLD* in bold black letters had been slapped diagonally across its face.

Its message made her start.

My God... Bryan sold the house while I was gone.

What could she do now?

Her thoughts looping, she stood stock-still, staring numbly at the sign, then at the front door, then at the sign again.

Had the new owners moved in yet? If so, what would she do if she couldn't get inside? And even if she could, how could she explain her actions to the new owners? Or to the cops, if anyone decided to press charges?

Should she continue with her plan?

She couldn't foresee any alternative. Her life had been in total shambles ever since she'd returned home. She'd come all this way to see Margaret Freedman again and ask for her spirit to be returned. To retrieve her life. To become the same person she'd always been. It didn't matter that Bryan had sold the house. Her problem remained, and the solution awaited her just on the other side of the front door.

She wondered if the people who had bought the place were inside right now. There weren't any lights glowing in any of the windows. That could mean that they hadn't moved in yet. Or that they'd retired for the night.

She moved closer and carefully pressed her ear against the door.

Silence.

Suddenly wary, she aimed the penlight at her wrist watch.

11:21. How could it be so late? Where on earth had the time gone? She'd left St. Clairsville right after she and Jodi had closed up shop. That was at 6:30. She'd reached Wheeling just before 7:00, and then Bridgeport no more than twenty minutes after that. That made it approximately 7:20.

Then she'd come out here, which took another half-hour, and—

The deadfall. Yes. That was it all along. It had taken forever to maneuver through it without tripping and falling on her face, or stabbing herself from its hundreds of exposed thorns, twigs, and branches. And once she'd gotten onto the dirt road, it had taken at least another half-hour to reach the bottom of the hill. Then, of course, the actual climb—which, at this time of night, amounted to another twenty minutes.

Would that account for the time discrepancy?

Even estimating the twenty or thirty minutes she'd spent sitting in the Honda before gathering the courage to get out and approach the deadfall, that still left nearly two hours unaccounted for.

How could any of this possibly explain—

Focus.

She needed to forget about things that really didn't matter and concentrate on what had to be done. Later, once she'd accomplished what she came to do, she could figure out what had actually happened.

She remained staring at the front door, debating with herself what her first action should be. It didn't take her long to realize that she had to take this one step at a time. And that very first step meant entering the house.

Then, amidst her inner turmoil, she noticed that she'd already approached the front door.

I can't help it, she reminded herself. *I have to do this. It's the only way to get my life back. And despite my fears and shortcomings, my spirit is guiding me to do the right thing.*

She kept moving until she was standing just two feet from the door. Then, as the fear set in once again, making her wonder if she could actually find the courage to grasp the doorknob, she discovered that she'd already done so. She aimed the penlight at her right hand and saw that it had already grasped the glass knob and had been slowly turning it.

To her utter surprise, the door eased open.

The foyer wasn't quite pitch-black. A small nightlight fixed to the wall near the foot of the

231

staircase illuminated the area in a dull orange haze. The door to her left, which opened to the dining room, was closed. The door on the other side of the staircase, which led to the kitchen and the short hall leading out to the patio and backyard, was also closed.

The only thing different was the collection of a dozen or so small boxes sitting against the front wall of the house, directly to her right.

Lynn stood frozen, listening. She heard nothing.

Confident no one was up or about, she closed the front door very softly and approached the staircase. After several awkward, panic-filled moments, she began climbing, using the outer edge of each step to avoid making creaks beneath her weight.

What if someone suddenly comes out into the hall to use the bathroom? Or makes a trip downstairs for a nighttime snack?

It didn't matter. This was necessary. No matter what the consequences. And if someone woke up, saw her and called the police, she'd just have to take it from there.

It took considerable time to reach the top of the staircase. For several minutes she stood perfectly still, her penlight aimed at the floor a couple of yards straight ahead as she anxiously gawked at the dark hall. Although she'd been in this very same place just a few weeks ago, she had the weird feeling that she'd never actually been here before.

Were the people who bought this place responsible for this strange feeling of isolation? Or was her imagination causing all this?

Is it because I really don't want to be here? Or because I've changed, experiencing sensations I would never have felt before I'd entered the Enlightenment Room?

Taking a deep breath, she aimed her light straight ahead, down the long, dark hall that led to Margaret Freedman's mysterious room.

Convinced this was the right thing to do and that she would find no inner peace otherwise, she moved slowly and quietly down the hall. Once she'd reached the halfway point, she pointed the beam to her right, where the Enlightenment Room would be.

And hoped no one had claimed it as their bedroom.

She took a few more deliberate, cautious steps. When she was less than five feet away, she stopped abruptly.

Someone's voice was coming from inside the room.

Lynn's pulse skipped a beat.

She knew right then that she needed to get out of the house. This situation had grown both weird and frightening at the same time. She was all alone in a big dark house and had no idea who else was there or what was going on. The only thing that made any sense was to turn right around, run back down the stairs and get out as fast as she could.

But just then, she heard the voice again. This time, it was much clearer.

"Lynn? Is that you, my child? You've come back to see me, haven't you?"

She backed away from the door and waited for her heart to settle down. *My child.* The voice was that of the spirit lady. Margaret Freedman was in that room and knew Lynn had come back. This told her that she should forget all about her fears and inhibitions. Just forget about them and remember why she'd come here in the first place. Margaret Freedman was the reason why she was here, and Lynn couldn't possibly leave without finishing what she'd set out to do. She had to open that door, walk in there and settle this.

However, the fear that had suddenly taken over had turned her legs into two immobile pillars of solid stone.

But in the very next instant, something inside her began fueling the rage that had brought her here, and she realized she could not let the fear control her or her actions.

I have to do this. I have to go in there. I have to end this, one way or the other...

No you don't, said another voice, this one coming from a different place in her mind. The same place where logic and reason lived. And, most of all, common sense. *You have to get out. You have to leave right now!*

I can't. I have to find out what has happened to me...

The woman in that room is a bad spirit, the voice insisted. *She has deceived you, forced you to do despicable things...*

It doesn't matter. I have to see her. I have to beg her to undo what she's done to me, to my spirit. I just can't continue doing these horrible things!

She has beguiled you into becoming just like her. You are under her spell. She is a spirit of a different world and can only work her evil, nasty things through you. She enjoys doing these things. She will not undo anything.

I have to try.

You will never succeed.

But I have to at least try!

Do you honestly think you can do this?

I really don't know.

Then why would you even consider staying here and trying to reason with her?

I was a good person once. I want to be as I once was. And all I have to do to change all this is—

All the determination in the world will not work. The spell this witch has placed on you is permanent. You cannot possibly undo anything she has—

Lynn mentally switched off the dreaded voice and reached for the doorknob.

Chapter 27

Lynn paused in the doorway, the slender beam of white light trembling in her hand as she nervously scanned the premises.

She saw nothing, heard nothing.

But she'd specifically heard a voice.

Well, hadn't she? Or had she just imagined it?

"Close the door, child." The voice was very familiar and seemed to be coming from the center of the room. "We need to have a nice long chat."

Still trembling, Lynn did as she was told. She remained close to the door, her light beam searching for the source of the disembodied voice.

"M-Margaret?" She couldn't believe that her voice still functioned. "Margaret Fr-Freedman?"

"Yes, my child…"

My child… After all she has done to me, she still is arrogant enough to call me that…

Her anger flared, vanishing her fears. Despite the situation, she struggled to maintain her composure. She took a deep breath and focused on the issue at hand. "You told me…to come in. Well, here I am."

"I've been expecting you, child."

More anger flared within her. Now she knew for a fact that this spirit lady was manipulating her. Why else would she expect to see Lynn again? Was it because she realized what she'd done? The harm she'd inflicted? The torment? The sadness?

"I'll bet you were," she said, a little more venomously than she'd intended.

"I sensed you coming the moment you left your store in St. Clairsville. This is why I made sure the front door was left unlocked."

"*You* did that?"

"It was necessary."

"But how did you...how c-could you—"

"I merely blocked the new owner's thoughts when he decided to lock the front door before retiring for the night. I did some shifting and had him concentrate on going straight to bed."

"You can actually *do* that?"

"I can still influence some mortals, dear. Especially when it is necessary."

She wanted to take issue with that but decided that there were more important things to discuss.

"Why don't you show yourself?" she asked.

"I'm very uncomfortable with this new family, child. I'm sure you can understand. Their hostility and negativity—well, it weakens me. Nowadays, I find it much more satisfying to stay within my little realm."

"Bryan sure sold the house awfully fast."

"The day after you left, in fact. He'd wanted a quick sale, so he shaved quite a bit off the final price."

"I'm sorry."

"I am, too, child. Although I live in a different sphere, this will always be my true home. My most treasured memories remain here. Which means I will also remain here, even though strangers now live in my house."

"We could have talked outside. Didn't you tell me that you loved being outdoors?"

"I still do, in fact. But this sort of talk is best suited for indoors. In this room, specifically."

"I guess that makes sense..."

"So then, why *did* you come back?"

Her question caused the anger to return rather quickly. She had to take a breath and collect herself before she could manage a reply. "You honestly don't know?"

"I have some idea."

"I came because...because you lied to me. Because you have ruined my life."

"How have I done that, child?"

The heat inside her grew even more intense. She took a few more deep breaths. *Mellow,* her inner voice commanded. *You must at least try.*

"You told me all about warmth and brightness. And wonderful, happy feelings. But once I left this house, everything turned dark and cold, and two people died after talking to me. They died because of how I felt, how I reacted to them. What I said to them."

"You let the darkness into your soul, my child."

"I couldn't help it."

"Couldn't you?"

The question unnerved her. "I went back to my apartment. My boyfriend came to see me. He was the one who tore my life into little pieces, and when I saw him again, I couldn't...I just couldn't keep my emotions in check. I was hurt and devastated. And scared and angry, all at once. I saw red. And when that happened, the darkness and the hatred also came back. And before I realized it, I told him to go away, to get out of my life. I told him—I told him I never wanted to see him again."

"And in doing this, you released the warmth and the brightness, and the darkness and cold rushed right in. And when you let in the dark forces, they gained a foothold. Once they'd triumphed, they sucked the darkness from your boyfriend and in no time claimed you." A strange golden glow appeared in the center of the room.

"As I just said, I—"

"You couldn't help it."

"What was I supposed to do?"

"If you'd have forgiven him, the darkness would not have been able to come in and take over your soul."

"I *wanted* to forgive him. I really did... I did later on, but it was too late. He was already gone."

"You are human," the spirit lady said. "You cannot help acting as your spirit dictates." The golden glow intensified; Lynn suspected that the spirit lady had come closer. "You cannot help how you feel. How you react. How you love and how you hate. As a human being, you cannot avoid being hurt, and when you are hurt, you react as only a wounded creature can act."

"I want my life back." Lynn was surprised that the words came out so easily. She hadn't thought she would have been able to say it at all. It seemed apparent that instinct had stepped in and taken over. She was passionate about her life, and that was the most important thing she could think of. Because, after all, this spirit lady had literally stolen her life from her.

And I've come back to reclaim it.

Shouldn't she at least try? Shouldn't this spirit lady, who considered her a kindred spirit, understand Lynn's torment? If Margaret Freedman was the benevolent, gentle soul she appeared to be, shouldn't she want Lynn to be happy again? To at least be as comfortable as she once was?

The spirit lady should have already told her she'd do it. She should have already told Lynn things would be better for her. That life would revert back to how it once was.

Lynn waited anxiously for a reply.

However, the heavy silence filling the room told her something she just didn't want to hear.

Lynn remained standing just a few feet from the closed door, her beam of light trained on the golden haze directly in front of her.

Then, finally, she heard the spirit lady's voice.

"I am sorry, my child. I cannot grant your latest wish."

My God... Did she actually say that? Did she honestly say what I thought I heard her say?

"Why not?" It took all her willpower to keep from screaming. From waking the entire household. It was all she could do to keep her voice down. "You *took* it! You *stole* it from me!"

240

"How could I steal your life from you? It was your life, child. I couldn't possibly have--"

"You lied to me."

"I did not lie to you. I told you everything you needed to know."

"You told me all the good stuff. All the terrific things anyone would love to hear. You didn't tell me what would happen if I acted human..."

"I told you the truth, child. I told you what you needed to know about the warmth, the goodness, and the love in this room. I told you that since we were kindred spirits, you'd absorb all the wonderful emotions in this room, and that it was all you needed to enjoy a wonderfully happy—"

"You told me nothing about the darkness. You should have, you know. It was something I really needed to know."

"I didn't think you would want to know about the darkness, child. Very few people do, actually."

"You should have at least warned me about it. You should have warned me about the anger. And the cold. And the evil."

"I didn't think it was necessary to—"

"I needed to know. I needed to be warned."

"And if I had warned you?"

"At least I would have known everything was not going to be wonderful and warm and bright. At least I would have been more aware of a flip side to all this. I would have somehow prepared myself. I would have suspected that darkness and evil were right there, waiting to—"

241

"Evil already exists in you, child. It is always there and will always be there. However, in order to grow and become functional, it must be summoned."

"Are you saying this *evil*…exists…in *me*?"

"Evil exists in everyone, child. But then, so does good. Every mortal since the beginning of time has walked with evil clinging desperately to his spirit. It is only the select few who are capable of keeping their own personal dark forces in check. When we first met, I had a strong feeling you were one of the few. I am saddened to discover that you are, at this point in your life, much too weak to resist it."

"But as you've already said, I am human. I have feelings, emotions. I'm not perfect. When I am hurt, I bleed. How could you think for one single moment that I'm perfect?"

"I knew you weren't perfect, child. No one is. I just assumed you were capable of keeping your anger and your other negative emotions under your control. But as I've already told you, I underestimated the dark forces lingering in this room all these many years."

Lynn's penlight flickered. Its batteries were about to die. She flicked it off and discovered some dim light coming in through the closed curtains. She studied her watch. It was nearly six o'clock. That was impossible. Had something gone wrong with the mechanism? She kept watching the minute hand doing its usual revolution. It was obviously working.

"It *can't* be morning already…can it?"

"It seems so."

"But I just got here maybe twenty minutes ago. How is that possible?"

"You have come to visit me in my own private element," the spirit lady said. "Things are much different here. Time itself is different."

"Apparently."

"It is of little consequence. The important thing is that you are here. And you have so many questions to ask."

"I believe we were discussing my emotions." Lynn told herself to stick to the main issue and not let herself be distracted. "Getting my life back so I'm able to live again."

"Just what would you like me to say?"

"I couldn't help the darkness taking over. I tried pushing it away, but I just couldn't."

"It wasn't entirely your fault, child. I obviously didn't tell you everything you needed to know."

"Well, I'm listening now…"

"It seems that I somehow failed you. I underestimated the power of the dark forces, and for this I am truly sorry."

"I don't understand. How could you possibly—"

"These windows haven't been opened for many years."

"What does that have to do with—"

"Everything in this room has remained here all these many years. Bits and pieces of every single emotion accompanying every person walking into this room. And when you first came in here, you absorbed tiny bits of everything."

"But you told me—"

"I know what I told you. I told you that, like the brightness and the warmth, the darkness also remains in this room. I also told you how powerful evil and darkness truly are. But as I just said, I underestimated the dark forces. How relentless they are. How desperate they seek escape. Freedom. Sanctuary."

"And the evil escaped? With me?"

"When I shared my gift with you, I thought the goodness of my aura would overpower the dark. But when I underestimated the negatives, I also neglected to consider the fact that once the darkness is let in, it is there to stay. The darkness is very powerful. When it gains a stranglehold—"

"I know. And it shows, doesn't it? Even that little boy I met down at the foot of the hill saw it."

"The little boy with a little gray dog?"

"You know him?"

"I've seen him many times during my walks in the orchard. I heard you asking Bryan about them. I've known for a very long time that everyone out here has succumbed to the local lore about my being a witch. I guess I just didn't realize that this latest generation already knows. Or that the very young are still afraid of what they thought I once was."

"Then the locals have no idea that you were a white witch?"

"Those who do not have relatives who were living here in my day have no idea. But what saddens me is that those who do have relatives I might have known have no idea what really happened. Who and what I was. How I helped people."

"I kind of guessed something like that when I bumped into the little boy the first time. He seemed frightened when he pointed to this house. But something strange happened while I was on my way here just a few hours ago. He must have seen or sensed something dark or cold about me. He suddenly grew very frightened. It was obvious he thought I was a witch. A bad one."

"The darkness has apparently taken hold of your spirit, my child, altering your outward appearance. I feel even worse now that I know I should have been more careful about the dark forces in this room. How dangerous they have become. How nearly a century of confinement has strengthened them, made them more desperate to escape."

"I told you, I tried getting rid of the dark feelings, but—"

Just then, they heard voices out in the hall.

"Who's that?" Lynn whispered tensely.

"The people who live here now. They seem to be getting up."

The fear came rushing back. "My God… What do I do?"

"Do you trust me, child?"

"What does that have to do with—"

"If you trust me, grab my hand."

The footsteps grew louder.

The golden haze suddenly vanished.

Lynn felt another stab of icy fear. "M-Margaret? Are you still there?"

"Yes, child. Grab my hand."

Lynn switched the beam back on and jerked it in every direction. She saw nothing. "Where are you? I can't—"

"Turn off the light, child. *Now.*"

Her pulse hammering, Lynn switched off the beam.

A fine-boned hand with long, elegant fingers and beautifully manicured white nails appeared brightly in the darkness, moving straight for her.

Lynn reached out and grasped it.

A warm tingling sensation made her shudder, and as it scurried up her arm, Lynn was immediately overcome with an exhilarating warmth. She took a deep breath and closed her eyes. The warmth shimmered inside her. She opened her eyes and shivered in excitement.

The room had disappeared. Myriads of glorious colors floated past her vision. Strong scents of honeysuckle, cinnamon, vanilla, lavender, ginger and sandalwood brushed gently by, invigorating her.

More colors drifted past, intermingling, turning everything into a masterpiece of brilliant textures. Sparkling light jumped all around her. As she bathed herself in this wonderful splendor, dragonflies and butterflies appeared, flitting about happily as the colorful wisps floated by. Several cardinals emerged from the clouds, their wings

246

fluttering. Then a few sparrows. Some blue jays. And more butterflies.

Completely mesmerized, Lynn felt a catch in her throat. "This is so...wonderful," she whispered. "This is simply incredibly beautiful..."

"Welcome to my world, child," whispered a soft, warm voice very close to her.

A beautiful golden and black butterfly emerged from a tiny golden cloud. Its wings fluttering, it skipped happily over to her right, where a beautiful figure in white floated just above the surface of the gleaming emerald green floor. It was Margaret Freedman. She was smiling brightly as she held Lynn's hand. Her large deep-blue eyes, reflected by the golden brightness of the white sphere directly behind her, were dazzling. Her white satin dress glittered with blue, gold and maroon sequins, and her long, flowing red hair glowed with bright flame.

Lynn could feel the fear vanishing. Warmth had quickly replaced it. And brightness. And a comforting sensation she hadn't felt before.

"This is your...sphere?" she asked softly. "Your...new home?"

"Yes, child. It is where I live now. It is the world I created while I was living in your sphere. A world of my own making."

Lynn realized in that same moment that she'd been wrong about this lady. Margaret Freedman could not possibly be nasty or evil. Only a beautiful soul could live in such a wonderful place. And bad souls certainly could not produce such a bright world…or one radiating so much warmth and beauty.

"I was wrong about you," she said. "I'm *so* sorry. I didn't mean—"

"I understand, child. It is all right."

Just then, Lynn heard a loud click directly behind her. She turned sharply.

The door squealed open.

Chapter 28

A teenage girl and a boy around twelve rushed into the room.

The girl immediately flicked on the light switch. The boy nervously scanned the room. Then he crept over and, getting on his knees, peered underneath the bed.

"I *swear* I heard somebody talkin' in here," the boy whispered. He jumped up and continued looking around. He wore a bright-red tee shirt with the number *51* printed in large square white letters on the front, and baggy charcoal-gray sweatpants. He was in his bare feet. The top of his head came up to the girl's nose. He looked like he tipped the scales at no more than fifty pounds after a heavy meal.

"You're a dipwad." The girl's thin sandy brows mashed together. Flat-chested and skinny, she wore a loose-fitting light-blue sweatshirt with a large print of Hugh Jackman's smiling face displayed prominently on the front. The sweatshirt went halfway down to her knees, exposing her slender thighs, bony kneecaps, and skinny calves. She was also barefoot. Her hair, a light shade of brown, hung loose, reaching her hips.

"What's *that* gotta do with anything?" the boy snapped.

"Just statin' a fact."

The boy kept looking around, tilting his head as if listening. He cautiously approached the closet, opened the door, and quickly stepped back.

"Boo!" The girl giggled.

He turned and glared. "Not funny."

She shrugged and pushed some hair away from her bony cheek. "See anyone in here, Sherlock?"

The boy didn't reply.

"See there? Nothin', right?"

"That don't mean nothin'. Heard somebody. Lady's voice. She was talkin'."

"To who?"

"I didn't hear nobody else."

"Don't that tell ya anything?"

"I'm tellin' ya, I *heard* somebody. I totally did."

"Well, *I* didn't, and I don't see nobody. This makes you a dipwad."

"I heard a buncha weird crap used to happen in this place." The boy's light-blue eyes grew. "We both did."

The girl shrugged. "Doesn't mean it happened. People are assholes. They make up stuff all the time. Makes 'em feel important."

"That don't mean a buncha crap *didn't* happen…"

"Too late to do anything about it now." The girl frowned. "Dad wanted this place so he could hunt for deer and rabbits without anyone bitchin'. So, here we are."

"Dad said he's gonna get me a rifle soon!" The boy's eyes lit up.

250

"Oh, goody." The girl looked nauseated. "A dipwad with a rifle. I feel so *safe…*"

"Lotta woods out there." The boy went over to the window and parted the blinds. A beam of morning sun sliced into the room.

Lynn stood frozen, gripping Margaret Freedman's hand as the girl came closer and then slipped *through* her while crossing the room. The girl shivered and stopped cold. Frowning, she turned and gazed directly in Lynn's direction. "Damn *cold* in here."

"*I* ain't cold," the boy said.

"That's 'cause you're a dingleberry. Everyone knows dingleberries always stay warm."

"Why's that?"

"They stick real close to assholes."

The boy cackled laughter. "You just called yourself an asshole!"

"Don't be a dickhead. Remember that last time ya pissed me off?" She held up a small, bony fist in front of her face.

"Yeah, I remember." The boy grimaced and rubbed his stomach.

"And the time before that?"

He rubbed the back of his head and nodded.

"Then bug off before ya piss me off again." She yawned. "And don't ever wake me up again—especially for somethin' stupid."

"This wasn't stupid! I heard somebody *talkin'* in here!"

"You're a dipwad. Even worse, you're a delusional dipwad."

251

"I totally heard someone in here."

She glared at him once again and looked around.

The boy scratched the back of his neck. "This room could be where—"

"Where what?"

"You know. Where all that weird crap happened."

"Yeah. Right. A witch used to live here. Bubble, bubble, toil and all that other totally stupid shit only a moron like you would believe."

"Some say she's still here."

"Yeah, sure. This place is haunted. A witch lives here. She's been livin' here for four hundred years and doesn't wanna leave." The girl looked like she'd just swallowed something sour. "Seriously? You really *believe* that nasty shit?"

"I dunno. And don't say shit. Ya know how Mum hates it."

"Mum ain't here now, is she?"

The boy began staring at the area where Margaret and Lynn were standing.

"This boy might become a sensitive one day," the spirit lady said.

Lynn couldn't believe Margaret had actually spoken while the two kids were standing there. She held her index finger to her mouth.

"They can't hear us." The spirit lady smiled. "Is that what you were thinking?"

Lynn nodded.

"Don't worry. As long as you're holding my hand, you'll remain in my sphere, totally

252

invulnerable to your world. Mortals cannot hear you. Or touch you. Or even see you."

"Really?"

"Are you surprised?"

"Very."

"I smell breakfast," the boy said, sniffing and grinning. "Mum's makin' pancakes!"

"Is that *all* you think about?" his sister asked. "Fillin' up that scrawny stomach so you can chow down and belch like a gross pig?"

"All *you* think about is that blond dude in English class." He grinned impishly and fluttered his eyelashes. "What's his name?" He raised the pitch of his voice half an octave. "Brad?"

"Don't you *dare* talk about him! 'Specially in front of Mum and Daddy!"

"Whaddya gonna do? You know Mum hates him."

"Mum doesn't have to know my business, asshole."

He scratched his jaw and looked pensive. "I guess I could forget about him, then…if I tried…"

"You'd better start doin' a whole buncha tryin'!"

"Maybe I'll just tell her about the time you and that other guy were makin' out behind the bleachers last month, and how Brad almost found out—"

"You'd better cut the shit, moron!"

"Maybe I'll totally do that." He grinned. "Should be really cool to see what happens."

"You do, and you're gonna have a serious accident!"

"I'm scared. I'm really scared…"

"You'd *better* be, dickhead!"

"I thought I was a moron."

"You're a *lotta* shit—*none* of it good."

"Sticks and stones…" He rushed out of the room.

His sister called him a moron. A moment later, she moved through Lynn and the spirit lady, switched off the light and slammed the door behind her.

"Let's see what they're up to." Margaret's face had turned grim. "I'm getting a very bad feeling about her."

Still holding the spirit lady's hand, Lynn followed her through the door and out into the hall.

Thirty feet straight ahead, the boy trotted down the hall, to the top of the staircase.

Just ten feet behind him, his sister rushed after him, her slender arms held straight out in front of her.

"She's gonna push him down the stairs!" Lynn couldn't believe what was about to happen.

"Any suggestions, child?"

Lynn didn't reply. Without hesitation, she let go of the spirit lady's hand and ran down the hall. The instant the girl was within range, Lynn reached out, grabbed her by the collar of her sweatshirt and jerked her back.

Just as the boy began descending the stairs, his sister was yanked off her feet. Her legs flew high in the air. Gasping, she landed squarely on her butt on the hard wooden floor just a couple of feet from the top step.

***

Dazed, the girl sat on the floor, gently rubbing her tailbone. Her eyes were wet as she twisted around and gazed at the long, dark hall behind her.

"Whatcha doin' up there?" The boy had stopped halfway down the stairs and turned around.

"*Shuddup!*"

The boy stared wide-eyed at his sister. "Why d'ya look so funny? Your face is all red and funny, and totally messed up—"

"I *said*, shut *up!*"

The boy climbed two steps and watched as his sister gazed down the hall behind her, where Lynn and the spirit lady remained invisible, their hands joined together.

"Didja trip?" the boy asked.

"Someone *pulled* me, dammit!"

"*Huh?*"

She turned around sharply. "I *said*, someone *pulled* me, you moron!"

He scaled another step and peered down the hall. Then shrugged. "I don't see nobody…"

Massaging her tailbone, she twisted around slowly. "Coulda swore I saw someone behind me when…when—"

"When what?"

"Oh, go stuff your face with pancakes."

The boy's eyes widened. "Think the *witch* gotcha?"

"Morgan, you're such a moron! I keep tellin' ya that's why Mum and Daddy named ya that. Just take out the G and ya got—"

"Moron's spelled with two *o's*, brainiac. Even *I* know that!"

"Just shuddup and go stuff your stupid pie hole. I've had enough of your shit for one morning."

"What should I do first?"

"Stick your head down the toilet and flush it." She gingerly got to her feet. After regaining her balance, she reached back and gently rubbed her tailbone again. Then turned around and gazed down the hall.

"Hurt much?" Morgan asked.

"Only when you're still alive."

"It must hurt a lot, then…" Morgan grinned.

"I can make it stop. All I gotta do is push ya down those damn steps."

"Not while your boo-boo's makin' ya move all kindsa funny…" He stuck out his tongue, spun around and hopped down the steps.

"Dipwad!" She carefully approached the top step. Then she stopped and turned back around one last time. She swallowed audibly and, gathering up courage, whispered, "A-Anyone there?"

The spirit lady smiled at Lynn.

The girl trembled. After a few moments, she said in a very soft voice, "I know someone's there. I saw your long brown hair. Well, whoever ya are, you're an asshole for makin' me trip and land on my ass. Ya hear me? You're a total asshole!"

Lynn and the spirit lady both smiled.

256

"I *better* not see ya again, you bitch. You'll be totally sorry if I do! I *so* mean it! You'll be *really* sorry!"

Just then, the spirit lady cleared her throat. Loudly.

Gasping, the girl spun around. Nearly tripping, she scrambled down the stairs, three steps at a time, gasping at the pain in her tailbone.

Lynn laughed. "That was really cruel. And *very* entertaining."

"It was much too tempting to resist. I was growing tired of her. She's really a very nasty little girl."

"She's that, all right."

"That was very, very nice, my child." The spirit lady's smile turned very bright. "Very admirable. Extremely unselfish."

"I just couldn't let her do something like that. Those kids are little monsters, but I couldn't let something that awful happen. At least, not while I was watching."

"Let's go back to the Enlightenment Room, child. We need to talk more."

Still grasping the spirit lady's hand, Lynn followed her down the hall.

Chapter 29

Once they'd returned to the Enlightenment Room, Margaret Freedman let go of Lynn's hand. Her expression was grim. Lynn couldn't help wondering if what she'd done to the bratty girl out in the hall had actually been a good thing. Maybe she shouldn't have interfered. Maybe she should have just let nature take its course. The brother and sister clearly shared an ongoing mutual hatred. Lynn knew all about sibling rivalry—especially during the last few weeks. Why should she or anyone else do anything that would change or upset the natural order of things?

But out in the hall, the spirit lady had seemed pleased.

So why am I worried?

Her answer came quickly.

I'm uneasy because this woman holds my destiny in the palm of her hand. But I really don't care how powerful she is or what she can do. I just want everything to be as it once was. I don't want a dark cloud hovering over me for the rest of my life. I don't want to have to worry about someone dying just moments after I've finished arguing with them. Or having a terrible accident after they'd said something I didn't like. I don't want to be forced to keep my eyes and ears closed, avoiding people for the next forty or fifty years, because I'm terrified someone will die or suffer a horrible tragedy after coming into contact with me. I want to live. And experience life.

The moment Lynn had finished with her thoughts, the spirit lady smiled. "I'm afraid I have misjudged you, my child."

"Misjudged me? How?"

"I have just heard your wonderful thoughts. You really are indeed a genuinely benevolent soul."

"Really?"

"Well, all I can say is that I've never heard such intense honesty. Such wonderfully warm feelings."

Lynn stared at the floor. The fact that the spirit lady could read her most intimate thoughts had made her feel extremely vulnerable. "I'm *so* sorry...I didn't realize—"

"We are kindred spirits, child. Our emotions— as well as our thoughts—can intermingle even though we might not even realize it at the time."

"I guess I hadn't thought of that."

"Please do not feel badly. You have not done anything to be ashamed of. The most wonderful emotions are those that have come directly from the heart."

"I guess I was just reminding myself why I've come here."

The spirit lady nodded. "I'm serious about how I feel about your emotions. And after personally witnessing your actions out there in the hall, I have to repeat what I just told you. I really have misjudged you. You are an extremely wonderful soul. You have a rare gift. You are destined to become a pure spirit one day. It might be a year

259

from now, or five years…or maybe even ten. But when this day comes, you shall have a very long, bright life ahead of you."

"Is this all based on what I just did out in the hall? Or what I was just thinking?"

"Both, of course. However, what you did out there spoke volumes."

"All I did was—"

"What you did was something not many others would have done in the same circumstances. Most others would have just stood by and watched. And perhaps maybe even enjoyed the results. You chose to act. And in doing so, you turned a potentially dangerous situation into something quite tolerable. In essence, you've spared two young lives of severe injury and a lifetime of a damaged relationship and deep regret."

"I just didn't want either of them to do anything really awful. My younger sister and I…well, we've had our moments, too. But I never wanted her dead."

"Not even after what happened between her and your—"

"No. Not even after that."

The spirit lady smiled. "Yes, child. You have a very rare gift. Instead of letting those two destroy one another, you interfered—and at a considerable cost to your own safety."

"But I was in no danger. You took my hand and—"

"The girl saw you."

Lynn sighed. "I kind of suspected that. But does it really matter? Since this whole family has no doubt heard that this house was inhabited by a witch, their imaginations will always run wild."

"You are correct."

"Hopefully, that alone might keep them guessing."

"Perhaps..."

"Just perhaps?"

"The girl was watching you the moment we clasped hands. Mind you, she has no idea what she actually saw, but that is inconsequential. No one will believe what she tells them about this. The important thing is that you saved them both. And as your reward, I must grant your request."

"You mean—"

"Yes, child. You have earned what you desire most. And if that desire is having your life returned to as it once was, then I must use my powers to reverse the spell I placed on you."

"Even though I failed so miserably?"

Margaret smiled. "You didn't fail. You acted as only someone like you would have. And in doing so, you didn't disappoint me at all."

"Even when my boyfriend—"

"That is a past chapter, child. As everyone knows, or should know, the past is permanent. It can never be changed. You must reflect on it only as reference to help you act in the future. And, of course, reclaim your aura."

"Really?"

261

"When I first saw you out in the front yard, your aura was displayed in three parts. Green, for compassion and love. Blue, for peace and serenity. And pink, for softness. Once you were brought into this room and exposed to its wonders, your colors were revitalized. But at the same time, you'd also absorbed the dark forces I had hoped had long weakened from this sphere. And when you re-entered your life and were once again subjected to its negatives, the forces came into prominence, your colors dimmed and turned murky, and I began seeing black and gray, and a very dark shade of red. And when these negatives began taking hold, I sensed disaster."

"You actually saw what was happening to me?"

"Yes, child. My friends went to see you several times. Briefly, of course, but long enough to see what was happening."

"The butterflies?"

"And, of course, my birds."

"I honestly had no idea..."

"Some think they are lost souls. Others, like myself, know otherwise. They've been my very good friends for more than a century, and they don't mind shedding light on things whenever they sense that I might need assistance."

"I thought they'd come to see me because I let in the light."

"Some of them did, child. Others saw the dark forces that had consumed you, and they knew they needed to warn me about it."

"I'm *so* sorry. I didn't mean to—"

"They were much too difficult for you to handle, I'm afraid." She smiled. "Now that I know you are much too young to face them alone, I must let you live the way you were truly meant to."

"Then...I'll have no more powers?"

"You will be as you once were."

The realization slammed into her. "Then I'll never...see you again?"

The spirit lady smiled. "I will say this, and I never want you to forget it. We shall always be connected. Because of this, I shall never be very far away."

Lynn could feel her heart lifting. "Never?"

The spirit lady's smile deepened. "Whenever I sense that you need me, I will come to you. You probably won't know I'm there, but I will help you any way I can. But once you leave this room, your life will return to the state it was in before we met."

Lynn could tell the spirit lady was telling her the truth. The woman's expression was sincere. But the important thing was that she knew that her greatest desire had just been fulfilled. She was actually getting her life back.

"I don't know how I can thank you enough..."

"You have, my child. You have shown me the sort of person you really are. And I am very pleased. Spirits such as yours are extremely rare. And if anyone deserves to become a white spirit, it is you. This might not happen for several years, mind you, but when it does, you will know it, and so will I. And I'll be right by your side to guide you. But right now, you have very different needs, and

263

since you have chosen to live your life in a normal fashion, this is what has to happen."

"Then I really haven't disappointed you?"

"Quite the contrary, my child. You have made a very old lady extremely happy."

"What happens now?"

"Close your eyes. I must do what is necessary to return you to your former state. Once the enlightenment process has successfully left your spirit, you will be free to leave."

Lynn sensed a rush of sadness. "Now I don't know if I'm doing the right thing."

"This in itself tells me you are."

"So then...you don't think I'm making a mistake?"

"At this point in your life, my dear, I truly believe this is the right decision for you."

"Then I shouldn't feel—"

"It is time, my child. Let it happen."

With a deep sigh, Lynn closed her eyes. The spirit lady rested her palms firmly on her shoulders.

The darkness turned cold, then warm. Images swept past. People laughing, kissing, hugging, whispering loving words. The brightness dimming, turning darker. People crying. Weeping. Sobbing. Teary-eyed smiles. Darkness. The sounds of sadness, of misery, becoming more distant.

Moments later, silence.

Then, finally, warmth.

As the warmth grew more comfortable, she felt the spirit lady's hands leaving her.

Lynn opened her eyes.

The spirit lady was standing very close, her beautiful blue eyes focused on her, her gorgeous face lit up in a bright smile.

"Is it…over?" Lynn whispered anxiously.

"Yes, child. The process has ended."

Just then, they heard shouting.

It sounded very close. There were at least three different voices. It was probably the new family coming down the hall.

"Our time grows short." The spirit lady's face had become tense.

"How do I get out of here?" she asked. "I really don't want to deal with these people anymore."

"It is of no consequence, child." Smiling, the spirit lady held out her hand. "We'll both be gone before you know it."

Chapter 30

The door burst open.

The two teens and a tall, broad-shouldered woman around forty stood in the doorway, staring at them. The woman had thick black hair fastened in large pink curlers and wore a loose-fitting red housecoat partially open, revealing a black lacy bra. She also wore a pair of very large fuzzy pink slippers.

The fierce expression on her lined face displayed both rage and impatience. "Why the hell did you two pull me away from fixin' breakfast just to come back up here and stand here lookin' like a stupid fool?" she demanded, glaring at the girl. "I don't see nothin' or nobody in here!" She quickly scanned the room and snorted. "Nobody! Just you two silly brats and me in this butt-ugly, sour-smellin' room!" She turned to the girl. "You see a damn *witch* in here, Priscilla? *I* don't see a damn witch. Just two stupid kids with wild imaginations. Two stupid kids that're gonna have to wait quite a spell before havin' their breakfast this mornin'!"

As the girl nervously tried explaining what happened, Lynn and the spirit lady stepped through them, left the room, went down the hall and descended the steps smoothly, as if they were walking on air.

Moments later, Lynn discovered that she was carefully inching down the steep overgrown slope. She couldn't remember leaving the Enlightenment

Room or the house itself. She guessed that it was because she'd been inside the spirit lady's beautiful sphere and wasn't aware of anything else. But there she was, slipping past the grove of pines just down the front slope. She was pleased that she no longer had to worry about that nasty family or what was going on inside the house. Her only concern was that Bryan Grant had sold the sanctuary of the beautiful benevolent spirit, Margaret Freedman, to a family of foul-mouthed idiots.

Once she began to focus once again on her descent down the hill, she realized that she was alone once again. That made sense, since the spirit lady had no doubt broken their connection and returned to her own wonderful world.

Suddenly nervous, she stopped in her descent and turned around. The morning sun had come out of the clouds to sprinkle the new day with a beautiful golden mist. Birds chirped from the branches of the trees. The sweet smells of flowers drifted over from the woods.

Even in the splendor of this glorious morning, she couldn't help feeling so alone.

A ripple of sadness nudged her.

She was on her own again. This time, without the aid of the powers she'd been given just a few short weeks ago.

As she expected, this frightened her.

She tried convincing herself that it shouldn't matter. She'd managed to live thirty-two years as a normal female, experiencing all the ups and downs life had sent her way. What made her think things should be different?

More importantly, what made her think having special powers would make things better?

During the last few weeks, she'd been directly responsible for the deaths of two people and knew that this would haunt her for the rest of her days.

Looked at the situation in this fashion, having such powers seemed very much like a curse.

So why did she feel so helpless now? So vulnerable?

Was it because she was alone again? Or did it have something to do with the spirit lady abandoning her?

It wasn't so long ago that Lynn had actually *feared* the spirit lady. Just a very short time ago, she'd even *cursed* the woman for bestowing a gift upon her that had caused evil and death.

But now that she knew exactly what happened, she realized that the spirit lady hadn't transformed her into an evil witch at all. She'd merely given Lynn powers she wasn't fully able to control. Not yet, anyway. Not in this stage of her life.

As the spirit lady had said, she'd probably be able to handle this later, if and when she decided that she needed a major change in her life. A change that might benefit her as well as the people around her. Only then would she consider such a transformation something she would desire.

But would she be able to contact Margaret Freedman when she wanted this to happen?

Would the spirit lady still be available? Or would she have totally forgotten Lynn over the years?

"I'll never be very far away..."

After all that had happened, she knew she could trust Margaret Freedman. The spirit lady wouldn't lie to her, wouldn't promise something she had no intention of fulfilling.

And what else had the spirit lady told her?

"Whenever I sense that you will need me, I will come to you..."

The wonderful memory brought a warm smile to Lynn's face. She turned and gave the house one last glance. *One day I will need you again*, she thought, remembering the wonders of the Enlightenment Room and knowing that no matter who lived there, the room would always be awaiting her return.

When that day comes, I'll come back. And this time, I'll be more than ready for my enlightenment.

Then, realizing the time had come for her to leave, she resumed her descent.

A few minutes later, she reached the bottom and started walking down the path leading back to the giant deadfall that would take her back where her Honda was parked.

Fifteen minutes later, she reached the path, slipped between the trees and started walking down the narrow road covered with pine needles.

Just a few minutes later, she turned the corner and froze.

Two large figures were walking toward her.

The Pozner boys.

Dirty and obviously half-drunk. One of them carried a small silver flask. The other was smoking a cigarette and studying the large glittering switchblade he held in his hands.

They were about a hundred yards away and then stopped cold. They appeared to be staring in her direction. Then, after a few moments, they began moving toward her.

Oh my God...

They've seen me!

The realization felt like a bucket of ice water tossed in her face. They were headed right for her. She was certain they'd do what they'd originally planned for her.

The Playroom. That had been their original plan.

Lynn trembled when she suddenly realized she could not move.

They kept on coming.

Closer, closer...

Very soon, they'd be close enough to grab her. And toss her to the ground. And pounce on her. And drag her down the hill, to their home, where they'd kill her once they'd finished doing what they wanted with her in their Playroom.

And I'll be forced to endure all this, because I'm totally powerless.

They both kept stumbling down the road.

Less than half a minute later, they were no more than twenty yards away.

Then, just as Shine focused on her, she heard a familiar soft, soothing voice. It sounded very close to her right ear.

"Take my hand, child…"

The moment she heard the voice, she saw something out of the corner of her eye.

The spirit lady's elegant hand appeared.

Lynn instantly grasped it. And once again felt the warmth of Margaret Freedman's benevolent aura shimmering up her arm.

The Pozner boys stopped cold. Both continued staring straight at her. Neither moved.

Although Lynn remained content, safe and warm in Margaret Freeman's sphere, she found that she could not move. But she quickly discovered that she did not want to. She closed her eyes and bathed herself in the warm comfort and the wonderful scents enveloping her. She realized that, as in the Enlightenment Room, while she remained with the spirit lady, no harm would come to her.

Finally, Smoke broke out of his trance and squinted up at the sun. "Bright day."

Shine was also squinting. The gash on his forehead gleamed in the reflection of the sun. *"Too* bright," he replied, scowling.

Smoke focused on the area where Lynn was veiled within the spirit lady's sphere. "Didja see somethin' right here? Little while ago?"

Shine didn't reply right off. He hawked a thick brown gob of spittle onto the road and wiped his chin. "Like what?"

271

Smoke shook his head. "Coulda swore I saw her again."

"Saw who, Smoke?"

"You know who, goddammit." Smoke gave his brother a quick glare.

"That bitch? The one that whacked us?"

"Yeah."

Shine shrugged. "She ain't here."

"I see that."

"Makes me curious 'bout that Honda parked down there. Near the turnaround. Whaddya think, Smoke?"

"Prob'ly one of those property dudes checkin' out things. Boundary lines, shit like that."

"Yeah. Since they up an' sold the witch house, they been sendin' all kindsa assholes in suits out here."

The two stared straight ahead, Shine taking another swig of his hooch while Smoke finished his cigarette and lit up another.

"Couldn'ta just disappeared. Right?"

"Right." Smoke glanced at the flask his brother gripped in his hand. "Whadja put in that last batch?"

"Just some lighter fluid, as usual. You know what happened, that one time I used kerosene…"

"I remember." Smoke exhaled a thick plume of gray smoke and wiped his eyes. He shook his head and kept staring in Lynn's direction. "Somethin' ain't right."

"We ain't gonna tell Ma we're seein' things, are we?"

"Shit... Last time we did that, she made ya quit makin' that hooch for a week. That sure got ol' Amos pissed at us."

Shine scanned the area again. "Mebbe we didn't see nothin', Smoke…"

"Mebbe ya jes' put too much lighter fluid in that batch."

Shine nodded.

"Go easier next time, 'kay?"

"Right. Just a cup. No more."

They both resumed their walk and, hobbling unsteadily down the dirt road, moved through Lynn and the spirit lady.

Lynn took a deep breath and turned to watch them. They kept on walking. After about ten yards, Smoke snuck a glance back at her. In his drunken state, it put him off-balance. He nearly tripped, bumping into his brother before he could correct himself. Shine turned back around for a moment, then straightened and continued stumbling down the road. About thirty yards later, they turned off to the left and disappeared in the wild brush.

Lynn stared after them. When she no longer smelled the sweet scents or saw the bright colors, it dawned on her that she was no longer in the spirit lady's little world. She looked down at her hand.

The spirit lady had disappeared once again. Lynn was on her own again.

"Margaret? Are you…did you leave me again?"

Nothing.

Feeling sad, Lynn told herself that she should actually be happy. Even though the spirit lady had gone back into her own little world, Lynn was confident that her kindred spirit would never be very far away.

"Thank you once again, Margaret. I'll never forget you."

A horde of butterflies appeared from the overgrown brush just beyond the edge of the road. They flew right over, swarming around her. Half a dozen flitted over to her shoulders, hopped off and landed on her arms. Two touched the top of her head, one brushing the tip of her nose with its gold-tipped wing. Moments later, the warmth that had enveloped her suddenly vanished.

One by one, the butterflies disappeared as well.

Lynn closed her eyes and smiled.

A soft voice coming from inside her said, *"Go now and live your life, child. And when you need to talk to me again, I will come and see you, and we'll have another nice little chat."*

Still smiling, Lynn opened her eyes. Her heart lifted, and she felt happier than she'd been in a very long time. Life was good. The darkness had vanished, and she strongly felt things would be just fine from now on.

Her spirit swelled with warmth and brightness as she walked briskly down the road, where her Honda was parked.

THE END

ALSO BY DAVID BERARDELLI

THE APPRENTICE
THE WAGON DRIVER
STEPPING OUT OF MY GRAVE
COLORS
AND DARKNESS FELL
AFTER DARKNESS FELL
IN ANOTHER REALM
BEYOND RECOGNITION
THE NIGHTMARE COLLECTOR
HIDDEN
BEYOND GUILT
A RIPPLE IN TIME
YESTERDAY'S JOURNEY
AWAKENED